HAPPY ENDING

by

J. STERLING

ISBN-13:
978-1945042188 (Inspire Magic)
ISBN-10:
1945042184

Please visit the author's website
www.j-sterling.com
to find out where additional versions may be purchased.

Thank you for purchasing this book.

Please join my mailing list to get updates on new and upcoming releases, deals, bonus content, personal appearances, and other fun news.

http://tinyurl.com/pf6al6u

DEDICATION

This story is for every single one of you who emailed me asking, begging, and clamoring for more of these Fisher boys. I hope you love the story and finish reading this book with a huge smile on your face. I know I did.

Thank you so much for reading.

WOMEN ARE CRAZY

Ryan

I COULDN'T STOP staring at my cell phone. The picture Sofia just sent me of herself made my pulse race and my dick throb. My woman was drop-dead gorgeous.

I would swear on everything holy that Sofia was even more beautiful carrying my baby than she was before she became pregnant. There's nothing quite like seeing the woman you adore grow round and curvy with the product of your love. I always knew I wanted to be a dad, but I never truly understood just how much until meeting her and Matson.

I loved her son like he was my own, and I was determined to make sure that I never treated him any differently than his little sister. Not that we knew what sex the baby was, but I not-so-secretly hoped for a mini Sofia, a mini angel. It was a concern of mine and Sofia's, one we'd stayed up nights talking about. We both wanted to make sure that Matson knew he was just as much my child as the one growing inside his mom's belly.

Thankfully, it never even occurred to Matson to be concerned about it. He was just excited to be a big brother. "Like you are to Uncle Nick," he'd said, and I'd felt like my damn chest might explode.

The only thing better would be making it all official. I'd proposed to Sofia at least a dozen times since we found out she was pregnant, but each time she told me no. The first time I asked, she was concerned that I was only asking because we were having a baby together.

"I don't want to get married because I'm pregnant, Ryan. They're two very different things—babies and marriage," she'd tried to explain, but I refused to listen.

"I bought this ring for you before we found out. I'm not going anywhere, and I'm not asking because you're carrying my love child."

She cocked her head to the side, bit back a grin, and narrowed her eyes at me. "Then you can wait until after the baby comes to decide if you still love me enough to get married."

The idea that I wouldn't love her enough to marry her was beyond absurd. It was official . . . being pregnant made women crazy. Well, crazier than usual.

Another time when I asked, she looked at me like I'd grown two heads. She flat-out refused to get married in a maternity dress and tried to convince me that they didn't even make them, even though I knew they did. I'd researched them already, but knew if I told her that, I was potentially risking my life by arguing. Pregnant Sofia was a force no one wanted to reckon with. Plus, she didn't want our wedding pictures to be me looking *all hot and perfect in a tux* while she looked like *a beached whale in white.*

Her words, not mine.

The other night when we were lying in bed, I tried to be sneaky and slip the ring on her finger, but the damn thing wouldn't fit. I couldn't push it past her knuckle before she realized what I was doing. I knew that once she saw the diamond sparkling on her ring finger, she'd never want to take it off. But she was so swollen, it only further proved her point instead of mine. She insisted that if she couldn't wear the ring, then she wasn't saying yes.

Women.

She claimed it was bad enough that her body would still be all out of whack in her bridesmaid dress for Frank and Claudia's wedding, and that if I loved her at all, I wouldn't ask her to do that twice. So I'd reluctantly agreed to wait until after our baby was born and Sofia felt beautiful enough to walk down the aisle to me.

I only prayed it would be sooner rather than later.

The desire to make this woman my wife overwhelmed all my other thoughts. She absolutely consumed me, especially after everything that had happened with her ex.

It wasn't often that I thought about Derek and the car crash he caused, but when I did, I got all choked up, my breath catching as my throat closed up. I could have lost Sofia that night, and the very idea of not having this woman in my life was almost too much for me. I hated thinking about what he'd almost cost me . . . what I could have been forced to live without.

"Dude. Wake the fuck up."

Nick snapped his fingers in front of me, and I blinked a few times and focused on his smug face.

"What the hell do you want?" I clicked away from the picture of Sofia I'd been staring at and put my phone in my pocket.

"I'd like you to join us here in reality where people are ordering drinks, and it's your job to make them." He swung his arm around, gesturing at the half-full bar.

"You make 'em," I growled, fighting with him for no reason.

"Nah." He spun and walked away, leaving me alone behind the bar.

Asshole.

I got my head on straight and smiled at the group of women waiting for me to take their orders as our older brother, Frank, walked in through the front door instead of the back.

"Finally," I yelled to him, even though he was ten minutes early.

Frank gave me a confused look, shaking his head as he walked straight into the office and shut the door.

I decided that both of my brothers were dicks today.

Six cocktails, four beers, and three shots later, Nick finally made his way back behind the bar. "What's his problem?" He nodded toward the closed office door.

I shrugged. "No idea."

We both stared at the door, willing it to open on its own. Because the truth was, neither of us wanted to have to go in there and figure out what was going on with Frank.

"I'm not going in," I said before Nick could suggest it. "I have a pregnant girlfriend at home. I can't deal with any more moodiness."

"Really? Pulling the pregnant-girlfriend card?"

I nodded vigorously. "Hell yes, I am. You just wait until Jess is pregnant."

"I thought Sofia was an angel," Nick said, his teasing tone sounding like Grant.

I missed that old man. He'd been spending more time with Matson's grandmother since he met her than with us lately. I made a mental note to give him a ration of crap the next time I saw him.

"Yeah, she was. But now she has a demon inside her. She's mean, man," I said, exaggerating a bit.

"Fine. I'll go in." Nick turned on his heel but stayed put for what seemed like an eternity, but I was pretty sure it was only a few breaths. He'd only taken two tentative steps toward the office when the door flung open and Frank sauntered out.

He stopped dead in his tracks and stared at us. "Why are you both looking at me like that?"

"No reason," Nick said too quickly, brushing past him and pulling the towel from his back pocket.

"What's going on?" Frank asked me.

I shrugged. "We were wondering the same thing about you."

He jerked his head back in surprise, then huffed out, "Nothing."

"Oh yeah," I said, injecting a heavy dose of sarcasm. "Sure seems like nothing."

Frank deflated with a hugh sigh. "It's the wedding. Between Claudia, her mom, and our mom, I'm going to go insane with all the questions they ask me on a daily basis. I don't care about the color of the napkins at the reception. And why are there three thousand different shades of white? Who did that? White is white. Just pick one." He sounded completely exasperated and out of his element.

"Wait until she's pregnant," I said seriously.

Frank and I looked at each other, then burst out laughing. We were half crazy, exhausted, or both. There had to be some explanation for our ridiculous laugh attack, especially if ultra-serious Frank was involved.

I sucked in a deep breath, trying to stop laughing and pull myself together.

Frank wiped at his eyes, his expression finally sobering. "I just want to marry my girl without all the fanfare," he said, and I knew exactly what he meant.

"I feel you. I'd be perfectly happy if we only have a dozen people there when Sofia and I tie the knot."

I'd hadn't really thought about a potential guest list for our wedding yet, but saying that out loud felt right.

Small and intimate definitely appealed to me. But I knew I'd give Sofia whatever she wanted, even if it was the exact opposite of what I did.

"If anyone will okay a private gathering, it's your girl," Frank said confidently. "Hell, she'll probably let you two get married in the backyard, and I'm going to be so damn jealous about it."

"It's not like you and Claudia are having some East Coast wedding with four hundred guests," I said matter-of-factly, knowing their head count of about sixty was considered small by wedding standards.

"It's not the number of people. It's the details. There are so many details." Frank ran his hands through his hair and blew out a breath. "We couldn't even send out the invitations without making twenty decisions first. They're just invitations. Send them an email, for all I care."

Trying to lighten the mood, I said, "When I get mine, it's going on my fridge underneath a superhero magnet, just so you know."

"It better," Frank said seriously. "Did you know that in order to even pick that invitation, we had to choose the size, the color, and the shape of the paper it was printed on? Did you know that?"

I gave him an embarrassed look. "I actually did know that."

"Why am I not surprised?" he said with a groan. "You're a damn princess."

It had been ages since he'd called me any kind of girlie

name. I sort of missed it.

Frank threw his arms out in frustration. "Did you know that you have to pick an ink color, because heaven forbid you simply pick black? And don't forget to choose a font type. Do you want it to be raised on the invitation, or printed flat? Should the time of the ceremony be spelled out in letters, or be in number format? And, oh yeah, would you like to order the extra square tissue-paper thingy that goes inside the envelope for people to throw away the second they open it? Don't throw away that fucking tissue square, Ryan, or else."

The poor guy looked and sounded exhausted. Just when I thought he was finished, Frank started raving again.

"All of that for one thing. One thing. And we're late sending them out. We're supposed to give people six weeks' notice, but we only gave them four. They all know the date anyway. We had to send out the pre-invitation invitations. What are those things called again?"

I wondered if this was meant as a rhetorical question, and if he'd murder me if I answered him. "Save-the-date cards?"

"Yes! Save-the-damn-date cards. They already know the date. The invitation is just a formality." He gripped my shoulder. Hard. "Do yourself a favor and elope. I'm telling you. Elope and save yourself."

"Maybe save that speech for Nick." I glanced toward our youngest brother, who was chatting with customers while wiping down the next table.

There was no way that Sofia and I would ever consider getting married without our families and Matson present. Especially after everything we'd gone through with Derek. Running away and eloping would be like a slap in the face to everyone who had stood by us, worried with us, and fought for us. We could never do that to them.

"You're right," Frank said, an odd note in his tone. "If anyone needs to be saved, it's gonna be him."

"What do you mean? Jess is great." My head swung around and I stared at him. I'd never heard Frank say an unkind word about Jess, so I wasn't sure where this was coming from.

Frank looked at me like I was crazy. "I only meant that Jess works in the entertainment industry. Nick will be lucky if he even knows half the people at his wedding. It could be more of a circus than a wedding."

The reality of his words crashed down on me.

"Better him than us," I said, feeling a little sorry for my baby brother. Even imagining that scenario felt like a nightmare to me. "But I don't see Jess doing that. For as well-known as we all are, we've been able to keep our personal lives fairly private."

I wasn't telling Frank anything that he didn't already know. By far, the biggest media blitz had come after everything with Derek had been revealed—from his betrayal to his mental breakdown and his stalking Sofia.

And then there was the car accident and his attempt to shoot me.

But our story was quickly eclipsed by other celebrity news, and things settled down faster than any of us had anticipated. I was grateful for that. The limelight was uncomfortable, especially since Matson was involved. He was too young to have to deal with notoriety.

"I'm just saying . . ." Frank let out a huff. "Jess might feel pressured to invite certain people, is all."

I clapped him on the back. "It'll be fine. He has us to keep him centered."

"You and I both know that boy doesn't listen for shit." Frank rolled his eyes.

"He'll be fine. And so will you. Your wedding is right around the corner, and then everything can go back to normal."

I hoped I was right. But what the hell did I know about weddings and turning girlfriends into wives?

Nothing.

Not a damn thing.

And we both knew it.

BEING PREGNANT SUCKS

Sofia

MY ANKLES WERE swollen and my back hurt. Oh my God, being pregnant with Matson when I was a teenager was way easier than being pregnant now.

Everything ached, and I was miserable. Aside from the grape popsicles and Italian food I craved, I could stomach little else. It was a disgusting combination, I knew that, but the love child inside my belly was destroying me. The fact that it was Ryan Fisher's baby was its only saving grace. I loved that man with every fiber of my being, and I couldn't wait to give him a child. And not just because I needed him or her out of me.

After everything we'd gone through, this baby was such a blessing. New life had sprung out of chaos and death.

We'd never planned to get pregnant so soon, but life doesn't always follow your rules. This baby was exactly what we never knew we needed. And he or she was so very wanted. The pregnancy brought our families together, strengthening an already solid bond. It had brought everyone closer, even if it made me physically uncomfortable.

And Ryan had been completely amazing throughout the pregnancy so far. He rubbed my feet each night. He talked to my growing belly, and he took care of Matson without me having to ask. The man was a superhero, just like Matson always said he was. Maybe Ryan did deserve a cape?

I stirred the pasta on the stove, making spaghetti yet again, and waited for the complaints as the front door flew open.

"It smells delicious, angel," Ryan said as he rounded the corner into the kitchen. When he saw me, his eyes lit up just as mine filled with tears.

I knew he was lying. There was no way this man could possibly stomach another bowl of noodles and marinara sauce.

He rushed to my side, wrapping an arm around my waist. "What's the matter? What happened? Are you okay? Do you feel all right?"

I sniffed and wiped at the tears now freely falling down my cheeks. "I'm sorry that I'm making spaghetti again."

He laughed. "Is that why you're so upset?" He kissed my cheek and brushed my tears away with his thumb.

"Why are you crying, Mama?" Matson appeared at my side, his forehead crinkled with concern as he stared up at my tearstained face.

"Hey, buddy." Ryan turned around and gave him a

high five. "How was school?"

"Fine. Why is Mama crying?" he whispered to Ryan, but I could still hear him.

"She thinks we'll be mad at her," Ryan whispered back.

"How come?"

"Because she's making us spaghetti for dinner." Ryan made a yukky face, and Matson mimicked it.

"Not again."

Matson sounded so crestfallen that it made my tears fall even harder. I hated disappointing my son in any way, food included, apparently.

Why couldn't I remember being this emotional the last time I had a baby? Everything about this pregnancy seemed so different. I felt completely out of control. My emotions were out of whack, my body was massive, and I forgot everything. *All. The. Time.*

"If you don't like it, I'll take you out for burgers after." Ryan looked at me and winked, but the mere mention of burgers made my stomach flip.

"Promise?" Matson asked, and Ryan nodded.

"If you two are done talking about me like I'm not here, we can eat. Matson, will you grab some bowls, please, and set the table?"

"Yes, Mama." He reached up to place his hand on my belly and spoke to it. "I hope you come out soon so we can eat other stuff again."

I stared down at my son's head and ran my fingers

through his hair as I came to a decision.

"Actually, you two go. Please." I took the bowls from Matson's hands and pointed toward the front door. "Go out and eat whatever you want. Just don't bring it home, because I can't even smell it at this point without getting nauseated."

Ryan looked between Matson and me. "Is this a trick?" he asked, and I laughed.

"No. I mean it. Go!" I shooed them away, but Ryan refused to move.

"I don't want to leave you alone. You're going to eat dinner by yourself?"

He looked so uncomfortable at the idea of leaving me all alone. Ryan Fisher was still, hands down, the sweetest man I'd ever met in my life.

"I'm a big girl, Ryan. Please take Matson for something that doesn't resemble noodles and sauce so I don't ruin Italian food for him forever."

"You're sure?" he asked.

I tossed a set of keys toward Ryan, and he caught them easily.

"I'm sure." I scanned his face, his clouded expression clearly communicating that he was torn. "Look, it would really help me out if you took him so I don't have to do it later."

That was all it took.

The crease between Ryan's eyes disappeared and his frown turned into a slight grin. "We'll be back, angel."

"'Bye, Mama," Matson shouted as they turned and headed toward the door.

My heart swelled as I watched them leave. I'd never get tired of seeing them interact. I never realized just how badly my son needed a father until Ryan came into our lives.

With the sound of Ryan's car backing out of the driveway, I sat down to eat what had to be my 589th bowl of pasta since Ryan knocked me up. After dinner, I cleaned up the kitchen and checked over Matson's homework while I waited for the boys to come home.

When they walked through the door with huge smiles on their faces, relief coursed through my entire body. I wanted them to be happy, and I knew I was making them miserable. After some family television time, Ryan read to Matson in bed while I took a shower and washed my much-neglected hair.

My feet were almost completely hidden from me now. I could only see the hint of toes sticking out whenever I looked down at my naked body. And I couldn't remember the last time I'd actually seen my vagina. I lost her first, and had no idea what she was up to down there or how she looked. Everything was hidden underneath my giant baby-making belly.

No one told you those kinds of things, like how weird it would be to suddenly lose sight of body parts you'd always been able to see. But they never hesitated to tell you how turned on you'd be. How pregnancy hormones weren't only a very real thing, but that they'd take over your mind like a sex-crazed teenage boy at times. Just looking at Ryan was enough to turn me on to the point that I was convinced he could see the want dripping down my legs.

With my hair towel-dried, I wrapped a robe around my body and attempted to fasten the tie around my waist, but failed. I'd outgrown bath towels weeks ago, and now I'd outgrown my favorite robe. I'd known it was coming eventually, but still couldn't stop the annoying sting that coursed through me as I added it to the list of things that no longer fit.

Groaning, I flung open the bathroom door and caught a glimpse of Ryan lying on the bed, shirtless. Everything that mattered before that moment faded away in a rush of desire.

I wanted that man. *My man.*

When I cleared my throat, Ryan looked up, his blue eyes locking on mine. His gaze followed the open fabric down my breasts and to my stomach, and lingered on my legs. He looked at me like he wanted to eat me up, even though his actions said otherwise. Ryan had become gentle in the bedroom, too gentle. I was starting to think I was going to have to go all Viking warrior princess to get him to have sex with me the way he used to.

As I walked toward him, he pushed himself up to a sitting position. *Perfect*, I thought as I moved onto the mattress and then on top of him.

"Sofia." His voice sounded strained as I straddled him, then slowly moved my hips, grinding against him.

I smiled when I felt that he was already hard.

"Don't you dare say it, Ryan," I warned.

He widened his eyes, faking innocence. "Say what?"

"That you're going to hit the baby in the head. That you think the baby will see your penis and be scarred for life. Or any of those things."

"But I don't understand how I'm not hitting him," he said as I narrowed my eyes at him. "Or her."

"You're just not, okay? You're not hitting the baby. Your giant penis is nowhere near your child, but it's going to be on the floor if you don't stick it inside me right now."

"Good God, woman, being pregnant has made you mean."

Just like that, the waterworks started as I rolled off of him.

"I know. I'm sorry, but please have sex with me. Why are you making me beg?" The tears refused to stop, and I knew I was being completely irrational and annoying, thanks to these hormones. "You don't think I'm sexy anymore, do you? Is that the real reason why you don't want to do it?"

Ryan's eyes grew wide. "Are you kidding? Have you seen yourself?"

"Of course I've seen myself. That's why I'm asking," I snapped at him, practically biting his head off.

My body had changed, and it would be ridiculous to pretend otherwise. My face was rounder, my hips wider than ever, and there was extra fluff on every square inch of me. I didn't feel the least bit sexy or attractive. No, I felt like a walrus or a hippopotamous, one of those large, ungainly animals.

"Sofia, you're stunning," he said softly as he reached for me. "You glow without trying, and I get hard whenever I look at you."

"Really? Even now?" I glanced at the crotch of his jeans, noticing the unmistakable bulge there.

"Even now. Nick yelled at me today because I couldn't stop staring at your picture."

Ryan's lips found my hand, my knuckles, and my wrist, then moved up my arm and landed on my neck. I groaned because every touch felt so damned good.

"I want you," I breathed out as he nipped at my flesh.

His lips were instantly on mine, his tongue pressing inside my mouth like desire was fueling him from the inside out. My mouth opened for him, my tongue searching for his.

"You're so beautiful, angel. So fucking beautiful." He kissed me again, his hands gently kneading my sensitive breasts. "Does that hurt?"

"No," I said, and his mouth moved to my nipples, sucking one inside and then biting it gently, eliciting a half moan, half scream from me. My hips ground in a circular motion as I begged, "Don't stop."

"I'm not going to stop until I make you come."

His words alone were almost my undoing. "I love that dirty mouth."

"Being pregnant has changed you," he said, teasing.

I reached for his neck, pulling his head again toward my waiting breasts, and he eagerly obliged my nonverbal request. I threw my head back in pleasure, loving every single thing this man was doing to my body.

His fingers entered me, curving and finding my spot. He worked them in and out as he traced a line lower on my body with his tongue. Lowering his head between my thighs, he licked, softly at first, then dived in like it was his last meal.

"Holy fuck." The thought in my mind flew right out of my mouth without restraint.

"Good, angel?" he murmured, keeping his mouth on me as his fingers slid in and out, driving me crazy.

"Hell yes, babe. So good."

I tangled my fingers in his hair and pulled him tight against me, praying he wouldn't stop until I came, which was going to be in about ten seconds if he kept using his magic tongue on me.

"I love you. I love you so fucking much," he murmured against me, still licking and sucking.

"I love you too. I'm gonna come."

My release crept up on me, slowly at first, then bursting with sudden ferocity.

"Oh, Ryan. Don't stop. I'm . . ." I moaned and

bucked against his face as my insides exploded, ecstasy streaking through my body like a meteor shower.

When I finally stilled after my orgasm, breathing hard, Ryan smiled as he moved his body above mine, the tip of his dick at my entrance.

"Stop," I said, and he froze.

"Are you okay?"

"Get on your back."

"So bossy," he mocked, but he did as I asked.

I positioned him at my entrance and lowered myself slowly at first. Then took him all the way in, as fully as I could.

"You feel amazing," he said, his eyes locked on mine.

I couldn't have looked away from him if I tried. Our connection was too strong.

As I rocked on top of him, my body heavier than it had ever been, I wondered if I was crushing Ryan with my weight. But he never complained or said a word other than it felt amazing.

Desire pulsed through me, and my need to have him hard and fast took over. I fucked him harder than ever, becoming a wild thing. Nothing was enough. I was insatiable.

Suddenly, something inside me ached, cramped, and I froze as the pain ricocheted through my insides.

"Sofia? Angel?" Ryan's strong hands gripped my shoulders as he pulled me off of him easily and laid me down on the mattress.

I tried to catch my breath. "It hurts. Something's wrong," I said through clenched teeth as pain ripped through me.

"Don't move," he said, and I felt the bed dip.

It seemed like no time had passed and then he was fully dressed, kneeling in front of me with clothes for me in hand. "Let's get you dressed."

"But . . . Matson." I forced out the words through my discomfort, not sure what I meant. It was hard to think straight. I'd never experienced pain like this.

"I'll call your mom," he said, but then I reminded him that she was sick and keeping her distance so I didn't catch whatever she had. "Right. Mariana then?"

When I nodded, he fired off a text to Matson's other grandma. Then he lifted me to my feet and helped me dress. I hated maternity clothes.

"Grant and Mariana are on their way."

"They were together?" I tried to sound playful, but it came out strained instead.

"Apparently," he deadpanned without any of the lightness I expected from him.

"Are you mad at me?" I had to ask, knowing the answer was most likely no. He almost seemed to be.

Ryan reached for my hand and rubbed his thumb over my knuckles. "No. God no, angel. I want to get you and the baby checked out, okay? I'm just worried."

When he kissed my head and his eyes turned glassy, my breath caught. If he cried right now, I'd absolutely lose it.

Moments later, Mariana and Grant practically burst through the front door. They hurried through the house and came to a stop outside our closed bedroom door.

Knocking softly, Grant asked, "You two heathens decent?" Mariana chastised him in hushed tones.

"Come in, old man," Ryan said, and I was thankful for the spark of humor in his voice.

"Oh, Sofia, what happened?" Mariana cried out when she saw me, her face creased with concern.

Oh dear God. I couldn't tell her the truth, that I was riding my boyfriend too hard, and now I was cramping and worried that maybe we really did hit the baby in the head.

"My stomach hurts. Cramps," I said, skipping over the details. Then I tried to stand up straight, but my body refused, and I glanced at Mariana in question.

Her silence told me everything. She had no idea what it meant either.

"We need to go. Thank you both so much for coming over. Matson shouldn't wake up, but if he does, tell him we went out for food. I'll tell him the truth later," Ryan said, snapping out parental instructions like he'd been doing it his whole life.

He wrapped an arm around my waist and started to walk with me. Apparently, I was moving too slowly, because he suddenly leaned over and swept me into his arms.

Grant held the front door open as Ryan maneuvered us through it.

"Drive safe," Grant yelled as he closed the door behind us.

I tightened my arms around Ryan's neck, praying silently that the baby was okay.

FREAKING OUT

Ryan

I TRIED TO stay cool on the outside, but inside, I was completely losing it.

Sofia needed me to be strong, I knew that much, but I was terrified that we'd done something to hurt the baby—or her. If anything was wrong with either of them, I'd never recover. Especially if it was something that could have been avoided, and my inserting my Tab A in Sofia's Slot B could have definitely been avoided.

I did my best to tone down my fear and worry as we waited in a curtained-off area in the hospital's emergency room. Sofia lay on the bed with me standing at her side, holding her hand. I refused to stop touching her, and there was no way in hell I was going to leave her side.

The doctor walked through the door with a smile on her face. That had to mean good news, I convinced myself.

"Hi, I'm Dr. Anson. I heard you had a scare," she said as she adjusted her glasses, her tone confident but calming.

Sofia nodded, her hand involuntarily squeezing the

life out of mine.

"Mind if I check you out?" the doctor asked, as if either of us would have said no. That was the whole reason we were there in the first place.

"Please."

The doctor lifted Sofia's gown and gently pressed on her swollen abdomen. "Do you want to tell me what happened?"

Sofia's gaze shot to mine, and I gave her a small smile. Her cheeks immediately flushed, and I wondered if she'd be able to get the story out or if I would have to tell the doctor.

"Well, we were . . ." Sofia paused and swallowed hard, so I took over.

"We were having sex and she started having pains," I said quickly and painlessly. Sofia gave me a grateful look and her face relaxed.

"Okay. And the pain, it's never happened before to-night?" Dr. Anson asked.

"Never," Sofia said, clearly more comfortable.

"And you've been having intercourse regularly?"

"Well, this one thinks he's going to hit the baby in the head." Sofia thumbed in my direction, giving the doc a wide smile.

Dr. Anson cupped her hand around her mouth and leaned toward Sofia, saying in a stage whisper, "They all think that." She gave me an amused look. "It doesn't happen, you know. You can't hit the baby in the head.

You're not scarring the baby for life. You're not hurting the baby. Trust me, I've heard it all."

"Then what happened tonight?" I asked, genuinely concerned.

"Everything feels okay, Sofia." She pulled her hands away from my angel's belly and covered her back up. "Sometimes this happens. It's perfectly normal."

"But why did it happen this time and not before?" Sofia asked.

"It could be from extra blood flow. Your body is swollen from carrying a child, and sometimes that swelling affects things that otherwise would be normal and painless. Maybe you tried a new position?" The doctor patted Sofia's sheet-covered knee. "But if you start to bleed, or if the cramping doesn't subside within an hour after it starts, you need to come back in."

Dr. Anson turned to face me with a small smile. "And yes, before you ask . . . you can continue having sex. You won't hurt the baby."

"I wasn't even going to ask," I lied with a straight face.

After we'd signed a bunch of discharge papers, I wrapped my arm around Sofia's waist and pulled her tight against my side as we left the hospital. I was grateful that nothing was wrong with the baby or my woman.

"You feel okay?" I asked as we walked toward the car.

"I do. Except I'm hungry. Again," she said with a groan. "I'm never going to lose this baby weight." When I laughed, she swatted me. "I mean it. He or she has me eating carbs like my life depends on it. It's crazy that I'm not craving meatballs, especially since I'm starting to turn into one."

I laughed again until she leveled me with a glare that instantly killed my smile.

"You don't look like a meatball, angel. You look like the furthest thing from a meatball." *Wait, what the hell was the opposite of a meatball?*

When we walked into the house, Grant and Mariana were both asleep in the living room. Mariana was lying on the couch, her feet propped onto Grant's lap. His head was back in what looked like a painful position, and he was snoring.

I shook him gently, and he startled.

"Hey." His voice was more gravelly than usual, and he rubbed Mariana's calves to get her to wake.

"You're back," she said as she sat up. "What did the doctor say?"

"That everything was totally normal, and it should be okay," Sofia said, but she didn't sound convinced.

"You all right, dear?" Mariana asked, the concern clear in her tone.

"It was just weird. And the doctor blew it off like it was absolutely nothing at all." Sofia shook her head. "But it didn't feel like nothing. It hurt."

Sofia hadn't admitted all that to me on the drive home. For the most part, she'd stayed fairly quiet. I'd let her be, assuming she was processing things or just tired.

"Should we go back?" I asked. "I can take you back."

"No, babe." She touched my shoulder. "It's just a little unnerving to be told that nothing was going on in there, when it definitely felt like something was."

"But you're not in any pain now, are you?" Mariana asked.

Sofia shook her head.

I blew out a relieved breath. "Then I'm sure it's fine."

"I'm glad you're okay, angel." Grant leaned toward my woman and pressed a kiss to her cheek, giving me the stink-eye over her shoulder. He knew damn well I wouldn't create a scene right now.

"Thank you both so much for coming over." Sofia gave them each a hug, then walked them toward the front door.

"Of course. Anytime, you know that," Mariana said with a smile.

"Matson didn't wake up?" I asked.

"Not a peep," Grant said, then placed his hand on the small of Mariana's back and ushered her outside.

"Thanks again." I closed the door and turned to find Sofia watching me. "You good?"

She nodded and waited for me to reach her, then took my hand and walked me down the hall toward our bedroom. Just the feel of her hand in mine filled my heart with so much love, I thought it might burst. I never knew that love could feel like this—so complete, secure, and safe.

I was the luckiest damn man on the planet, and I knew it.

LAND MINES

Ryan

THE BAR WAS fairly empty the next day as I filled my brothers in on the scare with Sofia. I'd told them both over an hour ago, and their concerned expressions still hadn't faded.

"You're scaring the customers," I said, referring to Frank's scowl, then added, "More than usual."

He glared at me, and even Nick refused to crack a smile at my joke.

"Like you wouldn't be the same way," Frank said with a grimace, "if the situation were reversed."

My stomach twisted. If anything happened to Claudia or Jess, I'd definitely be as freaked out as my brothers. But before I could tell Frank as much, he pointed a finger at me.

"You have no idea what it felt like when we learned that Derek almost shot you."

I hadn't expected those words. Taken aback, I cocked my head to the side and met his hard gaze.

"It's almost like we have some kind of PTSD or something," Nick said.

"He's right." Frank nodded in agreement. "Just hearing you talk about Sofia and the hospital . . . it all came rushing back. The feelings of that night."

Derek was the last thing I expected either of them to be thinking about. I had no idea that what happened with him still haunted my brothers, but of course that made sense. At first, we talked about it until we were all blue in the face, but not so much anymore. It hadn't been brought up in a while.

"You could have died, Ryan," Nick said. "I think about that all the time."

"You do?" I asked almost incredulously.

"Hell yes I do," he said, sounding both hurt and annoyed. "So many things could have gone wrong. What if the cops hadn't gotten there in time. If Frank hadn't had the foresight to call them. If Derek hadn't just taken one shot. We would have never recovered from losing you. And I had no idea any of it was even going on."

I tried to keep up with Nick's rambling thought process and logic, but I was confused by his last statement. "What do you mean, you had no idea?"

Nick swallowed hard, getting a little emotional. "There wasn't a single part of me that tingled with awareness that something was off. I'd been home with Jess, probably happy as hell doing whatever we were doing. But the point is that I didn't know. I didn't sense anything. And you could have been shot and killed!"

"How could you have known?" Frank's tone was all

business, but his expression had gentled in sensitivity to Nick's feelings.

Our baby brother flung his hands wide. "Don't you think we should know when something's wrong with one of us? Like some kind of sixth sense, a tingling in your gut?"

I shrugged. I'd never really thought about it. "I don't know, Nick. It's not like we're not triplets."

"But we're brothers," Nick insisted. "And we're close. I just assumed that if a life-or-death situation was going on with one of us, we'd all know it somehow. I'm mad that I didn't know. I feel like I failed you."

Frank frowned. "How long have you been keeping this in?"

"It's not like that," Nick said as rolled his eyes. "I have a lot of thoughts about what happened." He shrugged. "They just sort of live in my head now."

I reached for his shoulder and gave it a squeeze, trying to reassure him. "You couldn't possibly have known, and you didn't fail me. What if the situation were reversed and it happened to you instead of me?"

Nick's eyebrows drew together as he considered my question. "Okay, what if it had?"

"Would you be upset at me for not knowing something was happening to you?"

He barked out a laugh. "No. You're not psychic. How could you possibly know?" He stopped short and released a long breath. "Okay, I get it. Point taken."

"But still," Frank said, "the mention of a hospital and Sofia in the same sentence might send us off the deep end for a little while."

"I'm sorry for that. I didn't even think about it," I said, and I was.

I was sorry that my brothers were still so affected by the night I tried so hard to forget, but never would. Sorry that we clearly hadn't talked about it enough, because it still lingered in our subconscious, ready to strike at any time.

"What's it take to get a drink in this shithole?" someone called out in a deep, gravelly voice.

We all turned to face a giant of a man who looked more out of place than an Eskimo on a sunny beach. He had to be at least six foot five, with a barrel chest and fists the size of cantaloupes. He was dressed in all black—black tee, black jacket, black slacks, and black boots, with hair and eyes to match. He looked like he was in his early fifties, age lines radiating from the corners of his eyes. Everything about this man screamed intimidation, and I wasn't easily intimidated.

I moved down the bar toward him. "What can I get for you?"

He narrowed his eyes at me, his expression cold.

I could usually turn the sourest of customers sweet in no time. But I wasn't sure this man had a sweet bone in his body, so I didn't bother trying. I kept my expression neutral, not giving him my most charming smile like I normally would with a difficult customer.

"Whiskey, straight. No rocks. And nothing shitty," he growled.

I turned around to grab our most expensive bottle. If this guy wanted to be an asshole, the least he could do was pay for it.

I set the glass on the bar in front of the stranger, who stood tall, refusing to sit. I cast a wary look at each of my brothers, who had both edged closer. This man looked like more than a little trouble, and we all knew it.

There you go, Nick, here's where our sixth sense lies—in sensing trouble when it walks into our bar.

The man glanced around, then took his drink and moved to the other side of the room. We all watched in silence as he reached out and touched the exposed brick here and there, almost looking like he was pushing every so often. Then he looked up for an unusual amount of time, and I wondered what he could possibly be doing since there were no ceiling tiles for him to count.

When he glanced back toward the bar, catching the three of us watching him, he let out a laugh that made chills run down my spine.

"What's he doing?" Nick whispered.

"Losing his mind?" Frank suggested.

I stayed quiet, pretending to dry the already dry glass in my hands.

"Who owns this joint?" the man demanded, his voice commanding.

"We do," Frank shot back, matching his tone.

"You three?" The man pointed a stubby finger at us.

When he reached inside the pocket of his jacket, my body instantly tensed, my mind racing as scenes of Sofia and Matson played in it on a loop. I assumed this man had a gun, and was about to pull it out and shoot us. I'd either seen one too many gangster movies, or I was more fucked up from Derek threatening to kill me than I realized.

When he pulled out an old piece of paper, I relaxed, even if my relief was short lived.

"What is that?" Frank asked as he leaned forward.

"Can't you read, boy?" the man asked, his voice snide and condescending.

I glanced at the paper, noting the word DEED printed in bold letters on top. "What's this?" I reached for it, but he slapped my hand.

"Don't touch my shit," he said, leveling me with a cold stare. "It's the deed to this bar—"

"That's impossible," Frank said. "We own this bar. Bought it from Sam years ago."

The stranger coughed out a laugh. "My apologies. It's not the deed to the bar. It's the deed to the *land* the bar sits on. So I'm going to need you boys to close up shop. You're not welcome on my land."

My blood chilled as it ran through my veins. When we'd negotiated the purchase of the bar from Sam White Jr., the son of the original owner, he'd never said anything about not owning the land it sits on. If he had, we would have bought both, because who wouldn't?

Why would Sam keep that from us? And why would he sell the land to this asshole who looked like a mobster, and the bar to us?

Giving the man a hard look, I said, "We're going to need to call Sam."

The stranger put the paper back into his pocket and folded his thick arms across his chest. "Good luck trying to reach him, considering he's dead."

"He died?" Nick asked.

"Couple weeks ago now."

Even though Nick never met Sam, he knew about the bar's original owners and namesakes. Sam Sr. opened his bar right after prohibition ended and kept it afloat for decades until his son took over. Then Frank and I came along and offered to buy it from Sam Jr. at more than a fair price. Despite the outdated fixtures, we saw the business's potential, and the location was beyond prime.

Since then, we'd updated most of the interior, but we kept the original name and some of the original fixtures. Frank and I wanted to pay homage to not only the family who originally owned the bar, but to the bar's history as well.

We knew a lot of shit went down here back in the day, although we had no idea what, exactly. Only random stories fueled by the Hollywood rumor mill and online gossip; nothing that could ever be verified. But this bar started as Sam's, and we were determined to keep it that way.

"This doesn't make any sense," I said mostly to myself, but everyone heard.

"We'll get our lawyers on this, sir, but there's got to be some sort of compromise." Frank's demeanor changed as he started to negotiate.

"I'm a fair man. I'll compromise by giving you thirty days to vacate."

"Thirty days?" Frank nearly choked, probably thinking about all the things we had coming up in the next month—like the baby and his wedding. "I'm sure we can work something out. We'll buy the land back from you."

The stranger laughed again, sounding more sinister than he had the first time. "No deal. I'm going to tear apart this bar brick by brick."

This couldn't be happening. There had to be some sort of misunderstanding.

"Why?" I asked, unable to imagine a single reason why anyone would want to destroy Sam's Bar.

"None of your damn business. And don't go sticking your nose where it doesn't belong, kid. It might get cut off."

As my brothers and I exchanged shocked looks, the man slammed a twenty on the bar top.

"Keep the change. You're going to need it, considering you'll be out of business soon."

"You can't do this," Frank shouted at his retreating

back.

The stranger stopped cold and turned back to level a hard look on us. "Thirty days, pretty boys," he growled, then turned and disappeared outside.

THE BAR IS OUR BABY

Ryan

NICK AND I turned toward Frank. "What the hell was that?" we asked in unison.

He shook his head. "I'll go call our lawyer."

"Is that even legal?" Nick asked, his eyes wild. "That can't be legal. That can't be right, can it?"

"Yeah. I mean, it could be," Frank said, sounding more than a little concerned. "I have all the paperwork for when we bought the bar in the back. I'll go grab it."

"It doesn't make any sense." I braced against the bar top, digging my fingernails into the wood.

"What part doesn't make sense to you?" Frank asked.

"That Sam or our lawyer wouldn't have told us the land and the business were separate."

"They did, remember?" Frank asked.

As I thought back to the overwhelming process we went through while purchasing the business, it sounded a little familiar, but I wasn't a hundred percent certain.

When I shook my head, Frank said, "Don't you remember when Sam said he had no idea where the original deed was? He assumed his dad misplaced it, so we had a new one drawn up that he signed."

"So then it's fine, right?" Nick asked. "If we have a deed—"

Frank shook his head. "If that guy has the original, then there's a good chance it supersedes ours."

Still thinking back, I supposed it was possible, even if it seemed farfetched. When we met with Sam, Frank and I had been ready for battle, assuming that he was going to take one look at us and laugh us out of the place.

I leveled Frank with a look. "He was so happy when we bought the bar from him, remember?"

"I remember."

"You guys didn't tell me any of this," Nick said, clearly angling for details.

Looking at my little brother, I said, "He said he'd had plenty of people trying to buy the bar before we came along. He told us that he refused to sell to money-hungry yuppies or crooks."

Frank let out a small laugh. "He said he knew it was a pipe dream, but he wanted Sam's to stay a bar. He didn't want someone buying it just to tear it down and build some *swanky hotel* or *stupid fancy-schmancy boutique*. His words."

I nodded, grinning at the memory. "And when we told him our plans to not only keep it a bar, but keep the name and a lot of the original fixtures, he couldn't sign the paperwork fast enough."

"He said we were just what he'd always hoped for,"

Frank said.

"Except that we were too pretty and young." I rolled my eyes. "And he hoped we were smarter than we looked."

"Sounds like another old man we know." Nick grinned, obviously meaning Grant.

"No kidding. I just don't understand how this guy could have the original. If that was even a possibility, wouldn't Sam have at least mentioned it to us?"

"Unless he didn't know," Frank said with a shrug. "I'm going to go make those calls now. You two do your best not to freak the fuck out in the meantime."

For some reason, his stern tone settled me slightly.

*

THE NEXT WEEK seemed to both fly by and to drag. I had no idea how time could feel so contradictory, but it had.

We still had no answers in terms of the bar, and the shady guy hadn't reappeared. The three of us did our best to calm our nerves, but the threat hung over us every hour of every day. We'd even stopped taking our usual days off, all of us wanting to be at the bar in case something happened or if he showed up again.

"Is Sofia giving you shit for being here all the time?" Nick asked as I lined up a stack of dried glasses.

"No, why? Is Jess giving you shit?"

"Nah." He laughed. "She's working a lot, so she probably doesn't even notice I'm gone."

"Claudia?" I asked Frank.

He shook his head. "Between her job and the last-minute wedding details, she's got enough on her plate. She realizes that I'm here more, but she doesn't ask why. She actually tells me to come here when I'm not being helpful."

"So, all the time then?" Nick said before I could, and Frank socked him in the arm. Better him than me.

I placed the last clean glass on the shelf and tucked the towel in my back pocket. "Have you heard anything yet?"

Frank shrugged. "Nothing more than we already know. It's definitely possible, but it would have been done so long ago that the files were never converted electronically. He's got a paralegal digging through boxes of old records in the county courthouse basement."

"Just like in a movie," Nick said.

"We're running out of time," I said, stating the obvious.

"Twenty-two and a half days," Nick said under his breath, and we all fell silent.

We were all stressed and worried, each of us in our own way. None of us wanted to lose what we'd built. It didn't seem fair.

My phone vibrated in my pocket, and I pulled it out to see Sofia's name on the screen.

"What's up, baby mama," I said with a grin, then my

breath caught in my throat at her words. "I'll be right there. Don't move. I'm coming."

My hand shook as I pressed END and looked at my brothers, whose faces were etched with concern and worry.

"Is everything okay? Is Sofia all right?" they asked.

"H-her water broke," I stuttered, terrified.

Of course the baby leaving Sofia's body was inevitable, but it was suddenly very real. Somewhere in my subconscious, I must have thought that she'd stay pregnant forever. Not only was the baby coming out, but it was coming out *today*.

"Get out of here. Go," Frank yelled as he shoved me.

"We'll call Mom and Dad. Anyone else?" Nick asked as I reached for my keys and headed toward the back door.

"Uh, Grant and Mariana, I guess?"

"Who's watching Matson?" Frank asked.

"Sofia's parents will as soon as they get to the hospital. You guys are coming, right?" Adrenaline rushed through my body with no signs of slowing down.

"We'll be there as soon as we settle up here. Go," Frank said.

At his assurances, I nodded. At least, I think I nodded. I couldn't feel my face anymore.

I raced home on autopilot, my mind spinning, my heart galloping inside my chest. When I burst through the front door, I found Sofia sitting on a chair in the kitchen with Matson holding her hand.

"Her water spilled on the floor," he said, his eyes as wide as saucers.

"It's okay, buddy. We'll clean it up later. Let's get your mom to the hospital, okay?"

When I looked into Sofia's eyes, she looked so damn calm, I was immediately centered. But I couldn't help but wonder how she could be so together at a time like this.

"My bag's by the door," she said softly.

"Do you feel okay? Are you having contractions? How far apart are they?" I spat out rapid-fire questions as if I had any damn idea what her answers would even mean. Sofia knew it too, which was why she laughed at me.

"I'm fine. But we should go." She moved as if to get up, and I wrapped my arm around her waist and helped her to her feet. "I've already texted my parents, so they should be there soon."

I nodded, letting her know I heard her. "Matson, can you grab your mom's bag for me?"

"Sure." He ran toward the duffel Sofia had packed weeks ago, placed the strap on his shoulder, and hefted it up. "I got it."

"You ready to be a big brother?"

Matson's smile grew wide. "Yep. And I hope it's a boy."

I walked my family out the front door and locked it behind us. We hurried toward my car, and I gently settled Sofia inside.

As we pulled out of the driveway, Matson asked from the back seat, "Do you hope it's a boy too, Ryan?"

I glanced at Sofia, who was breathing a little faster than usual, and squeezing my hand like she wanted to cut off all the circulation in it.

Do I want a boy?

"I don't know," I said, answering him honestly.

Of course, I'd thought about it over the past several months, but I'd never come to a firm conclusion in my mind or heart. All I knew was that I wanted a healthy baby with the woman I loved. It was a fucking cliché and everyone said it, but it was the truth.

"Well, I want a little brother. I mean, I'll be okay if it's a girl, but I want brothers like you."

And there it was. Matson wanted to have what he had become familiar with. He wanted brothers just like mine.

I thought about what he said as I navigated the streets as quickly, efficiently, and safely as I could. Sofia moaned once and it almost tore me apart. Her grip on my hand tightened, and I pressed the gas pedal a little harder. Knowing she was in pain wasn't something I'd ever be okay with, no matter what caused it.

"You know what, though?" I said to Matson. "I always wished that we had a sister too."

"You did? Like instead of Nick?" he asked, and Sofia and I both laughed.

"No, not instead. I still wanted Nick and Frank, but I wanted a little sister too. I wanted to have someone to protect. And I wanted to be able to beat up the boys who liked her."

"Really, babe?" Sofia said with a soft smile.

"I can do that if I have a sister? Beat up the boys who like her and not get in trouble?"

Matson sounded a little too excited, and Sofia's grip on my hand was no longer about the contractions, but a warning about my response.

"Great job," she whispered from beside me, and I bit back a smile.

It was the truth. I had always wanted that. How did that make me the bad guy? I figured it made me a good potential older brother.

"Maybe," I said, and Sofia immediately let go of my hand. Apparently, that had been the wrong answer.

"I guess a baby sister won't be so bad then," Matson said as I pulled into the hospital's emergency parking lot. Thankfully, I found an empty spot near the entrance.

I shut off the engine and ran around to Sofia's door to help her out. I tried to hustle her toward the entrance, but she refused to take another step, almost causing me to trip over my own damn feet.

"Ryan, stop. Matson!" she shouted.

I could have smacked myself. I looked behind us to see Matson struggling to keep up, his mom's overnight bag half as large as he was.

"Sorry, buddy." I hurried back and removed the strap from his small shoulder, then slid it over mine.

"It's okay. You were distracted."

"It's not okay," I said. The last thing I wanted was for Matson to feel replaced or forgotten. He'd already forgiven me, I could tell, but I still wanted to kick myself.

He ran to his mother's side and reached for her hand. "How are you, Mama?"

"I'm good," she said, and he beamed up at her like she was his entire world. "How are you?"

"I'm good too." He dropped her hand and ran toward the doors. "I see Grandma and Papa!"

I kissed the side of Sofia's head and watched Matson run into his grandpa's arms, thinking about how this would be his last day as the only child.

"You ready for this?" Sofia asked me with a wicked grin, like she knew something I didn't.

"You trying to scare me, angel?"

She laughed instead of answering as we walked through the doors, knowing when we walked back out, our lives would be changed forever.

APPLE STEM
Sofia

"**I**'M GOING TO kill you, Ryan," I screamed through the pain, and I meant it. "I can't believe I let you do this to me."

I looked into his stupid perfect face and wanted to hit it. Those blue eyes that I usually loved so much? I now wanted to gouge them out.

Fine. I was being a bit dramatic and I knew it, but you try pushing a bowling ball out of your vagina with no epidural and see how kind and loving you feel.

Why on earth had I wanted to have this baby naturally? It didn't make me any more or less of a mom to give birth with no pain meds, but for whatever reason, I'd convinced myself that it would be a nice thing to experience.

A nice thing to experience? It was funny how quickly we forgot the pain of childbirth, considering many of us continued to put ourselves in this position over and over again.

"I love you, angel," Ryan said, his voice so sugary sweet that he was lucky I didn't puke on his shoes.

"I might love you after this thing is out of me," I growled, and Ryan laughed.

He actually had the nerve to laugh. I narrowed my eyes at him.

"This isn't funny, Ryan. You have no idea what this feels like." Scowling, I squeezed his hand as hard as I could.

"I could never do what you're doing. I'm not laughing at you, angel. I'm in fucking awe of you."

I started to cry. Whether it was from his words, the way he was looking at me like I was a goddess, or the intense pain, I couldn't be sure. But as my tears fell, Ryan wiped them away and kissed my cheek.

"You are literally the most beautiful woman I've ever seen in my life."

"Shut . . . up."

He smiled again. My stupid boyfriend was clueless.

"I need you to start pushing, Sofia."

The doctor's voice cut through the rest of the noise, and I became hyperfocused on her. I listened to her count me down.

Ryan's hand was in my grip, like it had been for the last five hours. I was certain at one point that I'd broken at least two of his fingers, but he was smart to not mention it. I might have threatened to break the rest if he had.

"Almost there," the doctor said with a lilt to her voice that gave me a brief reprieve. When the slicing pain became my focus again, she ordered, "Keep pushing," and I did.

I pushed with all my strength and every muscle until I felt a slight sense of relief. The hard part of delivery was over as the baby's shoulders moved through. My entire body sagged, and I waited to hear the sweet sound of a newborn baby's cry fill the air. When it did, I sucked in a breath of my own.

"You did so good." Ryan looked at me with tears rolling down his face. "That was amazing. You're amazing."

I stared into the eyes that only moments ago I wanted to stab from his face, and I fell in love with him all over again.

Having a child together bonded you, made the love between you grow in ways you never thought possible. I had never realized that until now. I'd missed that kind of connection the first time around with Matson. There was no man by my side holding my hand then, telling me I was amazing and looking at me like I'd hung the moon. There was no one telling me he loved me and wanted to spend the rest of his life with me.

I'd been alone then. But I wasn't alone anymore.

"Ryan, Sofia, meet your daughter." The nurse handed the baby, who had been cleaned and swaddled, over to my waiting arms.

I looked into her perfect tiny face and openly wept. She was perfect.

"She looks like you," I said, meeting Ryan's blue eyes that were now bright with tears.

He leaned down to kiss me, then placed a gentle kiss on our daughter's forehead. We stayed like for a few moments, the three of us soaking in the moment like magic.

Ryan shifted his weight. "Should I get everyone?" he asked the nurses.

"It's up to your wife," one of them said, and my heart skipped a beat.

I hadn't agreed to marry Ryan yet, but I knew I would. The next time he asked, I'd say yes with no hesitation. I wanted to be his wife, and a part of me hated that I'd made him wait.

Right now, as we stared together at the precious baby girl we'd created, I wished that I shared his last name as we'd brought her into this world. I always assumed that I'd never drop my maiden name since Matson had it as well, but once Ryan talked about adopting him, all that changed. The four of us would be Fishers, something I never even considered a possibility until Ryan came into my life.

It seemed so simple, something insignificant in this day and age, but it was a bigger deal to me than I'd expected. Sharing Ryan's last name was something I found myself desperate to do, and I hoped he asked me to marry him again soon. The last time he asked would be the last time I told him no.

"Did you hear that, angel? It's up to you, my wife." Ryan winked, and I couldn't help but smile at him.

"Matson first," I said. "And by himself, please."

Ryan nodded, then stepped outside the room.

I looked down at the sweet girl on my chest, tracing her little features gently with a fingertip as she wavered between staring up at me and falling asleep.

It felt like Ryan had only been gone two seconds, and then he was back at my side with my first love, my son.

"Can I touch her?" Matson asked as he scooted onto the bed next to me.

"Of course you can."

Not entirely sure what to do, he petted her head as if she were a puppy. I stopped myself from giggling, but it was sweet. She was so tiny in comparison to him, and I flashed back to when Matson was first born and how quickly the time had passed. How was my sweet baby already ten years old?

"She's so little," he whispered.

I smiled at him and kissed his cheek. "I know. You were that little once too."

"That's weird." Matson hopped off the bed. "I can hold her when she's awake, right?"

I glanced down and noticed that she had fallen asleep. "Of course you can," I said, and his face lit up.

"You're not disappointed it's a girl?" Ryan asked, and Matson turned to look at him.

"Nah. I get to beat people up, remember?" Matson

said the words so matter-of-factly that there was no arguing with him.

I shot Ryan a look that told him he was going to have to deal with that later, and he just shrugged.

"Want to go get everyone else for me?" Ryan asked Matson.

"They can come in now?" My son looked at me for permission, and when I nodded, his expression filled with concern. "It's a lot of people, Mama."

"It's okay. They're all family," I said, and the words hit me like the force of a wave. This was my family now. Ryan's brothers and their soon-to-be wives, his parents, and even Grant.

They filed in one at a time, filling the room, and each person took their turn cooing at the baby. Once everyone else had seen her, Ryan took her from my arms and held her for the first time.

He was nervous, concerned with holding her head properly, and my heart grew a little as I watched my mom show him how. Seeing Ryan Fisher holding our baby in his arms wasn't something I was sure I'd ever get used to. I wanted a picture of it so badly, but my phone was God knows where.

Thankfully, Jess and Claudia both apparently read my mind. Each of them smiled at me, then pulled out their phones and took a few pics. I mouthed *thank you* to them, and they gave me a thumbs-up like it was something they'd planned.

"You've all been asking what her name is. So without further ado, I'd like you all to meet Apple Stem Fisher," Ryan said with a grin.

My mom's eyes widened comically, and his brothers' expressions froze before they attempted to form normal smiles.

"Oh, that's a lovely name," Ryan's mom lied.

Then Ryan lost all control and started cracking up. "You should have seen your faces," he said through his laughter.

Frank punched him in the arm, and I couldn't even blame him. Ryan deserved it.

"Who does that?" Nick said, shaking his head.

"What's her real name?" Frank practically growled.

"Hope." Ryan beamed at them, looking like the proudest dad on the planet.

"Now that's a beautiful name," my mom said, tears filling her eyes as she reached for the baby.

And it was. A beautiful name for a beautiful girl. She looked exactly like Ryan with the exception of her mouth and hair. Those lips were all mine.

"How'd you choose?" Ryan's mom asked as she took a few pictures with her cell phone of Hope with my mom.

"We kept trying to pick a name before we even knew her," Ryan said, and I interrupted with a small laugh.

"It wasn't working."

"It wasn't." Ryan chuckled. "We couldn't agree on girl or boy names, and nothing felt right."

"So Ryan suggested we wait. He said we were trying too hard to name a baby we didn't even know yet."

The room filled with the sound of sweet sighs of understanding.

"It makes sense, right?" Ryan asked, and everyone agreed. "She's the miracle we never expected," he said, looking directly at me.

"She's the light that came out of the dark," I added.

"She was our hope without even trying." Ryan looked between me and the baby, his eyes welling with emotion, and I wiped at my own, which had started tearing up as well.

Jess took a step closer, stopping next to my bed to wrap her arm around Matson, who was at my side. He followed suit, putting his arm around her. His crush hadn't subsided, and I dreaded the day she married Nick, fearing that my boy might get his first taste of a broken heart.

"She's so perfect, Sof. Congratulations."

"Thank you, Jess. Your turn," I teased, and the blood drained from her face.

"Not yet," she choked out, and I laughed, knowing that everyone in the room couldn't help but overhear us.

"I think someone might have cold feet, Nick." I glanced at him and nodded toward Jess, and he waved me off. The last thing in the world Nick Fisher was worried about was his status with his girlfriend.

"My baby's just trying to climb that corporate ladder

before she starts birthing future CEOs." He grinned and gave her a wink. I swore Jess melted a little with the gesture.

Nick and Jess always acted like a couple who had just gotten together instead of one who had been together for years, and I envied that. I hoped that Ryan and I never let our relationship grow stale. It required work to not get into that comfortable state where you expected things and stopped appreciating them, but it was possible. I wanted to make sure we both did that for each other . . . always.

"You'll be okay, right? For the wedding?"

Claudia had replaced Jess at my side, and I cocked my head to the side at her question. I knew she wasn't asking out of concern or worry for herself. She was genuinely about me being comfortable and ready to be a bridesmaid on her big day.

"Yes," I said enthusiastically, wanting to be sure she knew how excited and happy I was for both her and Frank. "Hope should be mostly eating and sleeping still, so the biggest thing I'll have to do is breastfeed or pump a few times during the day. I hope that's okay."

"Are you kidding? Of course that's okay." Claudia leaned down and gave me a hug.

"When do you think you and Frank will have kids?" I whispered so the eavesdropping group surrounding us wouldn't hear.

"Tomorrow." Claudia grinned as she glanced at Frank, who was completely oblivious to our conversation.

He was staring at Ryan and Hope with what looked like awe and maybe envy in his eyes. "But, seriously, look at him right now. He's going to have baby fever more than I do. Probably try to put a baby in me the second we get home."

"You might be right."

Frank looked over at us then and gave Claudia a smile that could stop any woman in her tracks. He was head over heels in love with her, and it was a beautiful thing to see.

"I guess I won't mind," Claudia said. "Congratulations again. She's really beautiful."

"She looks just like Ryan." I shook my head. "It's like I didn't even make her at all."

"Damn Fisher genes."

I shrugged. "Could be worse."

"Oh, it could definitely be worse. The three of us are pretty lucky," she said.

I agreed, even though I wasn't entirely sure what I was agreeing to. Were we lucky that our kids might be as handsome as their fathers? Or were we lucky that we were the women that they'd chosen to love and spend their lives with?

Maybe none of it was luck at all. Maybe all of it was?

I had no idea, but I sure was thankful for all of it.

DIAPERS ARE DUMB

Ryan

FRANK PULLED ME aside at the hospital while everyone else was ogling the baby. "I know it's not the best time to tell you, but I got some news."

"What did you find out?"

He pulled at his hair, which told me the answer wasn't good. "If that guy has the original deed to the land, then the one our lawyers drew up and Sam signed isn't valid. An original documented deed with signatures supersedes all others that came after."

My heart, which had been soaring on cloud nine only moments ago, came crashing down. "So we're screwed? We have no rights?"

"Technically, it looks that way. But I'm not giving up yet."

"Don't," I said firmly. "There's got to be some kind of loophole."

"Exactly what I was thinking."

We three were all financially set for life, thanks to not only the success of the bar itself, but also to the location fees we received whenever the bar was used in a television episode. Yet it wasn't about the money.

Sam's Bar had evolved from a dream to a reality, and Frank and I made it happen together without anyone else's help. And as soon as Nick joined us, it felt like even more of an accomplishment. The bar was about us as brothers being in business together, succeeding by pooling our individual talents.

Before Nick came along, we had allowed a few reality TV shows to film us for the free exposure it gave us. Nick was the one who changed all that, negotiating location fees for us anytime the bar was either mentioned or used as a shooting location. And if one of us appeared in the episode, we got a talent fee.

Those fees added up nicely over the years, continuing to earn us money without any effort. Sam's had become a part of us, our heart, and Fishers didn't walk away from the things they loved.

We had to figure it out.

*

THE NEXT TEN days passed by in a blink. We still weren't completely sure what the hell was going on with the original deed to the land or how this man could have gotten his hands on it. Frank's information so far had been deemed accurate, but we still didn't have any concrete information beyond that.

No one could find any records of Sam Sr. passing the

land to a new owner, but that didn't mean that it hadn't happened. There were apparently hundreds of unorganized boxes of property transactions to go through by hand, and that required time that we didn't have.

Because we had no way to get in touch with the scary dude who had threatened to take it all from us, we were at his mercy, which wasn't something any of us were used to. By not giving us a way to contact him, he'd taken away our ability to negotiate or get more information to determine what it was he was truly after. None of us could figure out why he wanted to tear down the bar, although we never mentioned it after we talked about it at length one night.

Like typical men, we refused to ask the same questions over and over again. What was the point when we had no answers? We'd just be whining like a bunch of girls, and Frank wouldn't allow that. So until we had a fucking solution, we didn't discuss it; which meant we never talked about it because we had nothing to offer on the how-do-we-fix-this front.

Aside from the bar, things at home were going great. Well, as great as they could when you no longer got to sleep through the night.

The whole *not having sex with my sexy-as-fuck girlfriend* issue had been easier to adjust to than I'd anticipated, but the not-sleeping part sucked. People weren't kidding when they said sleep would become a thing of the past after you had a baby. Hope woke up wailing every two hours on the dot, and Sofia was like a damn psychic, knowing exactly what the baby needed and tending to it, sometimes with her eyes half-closed. How she knew these things while I still fumbled a putting the diaper on properly was beyond me.

While I tried to spend most of my time at home, I also continued to check in at the bar. Since Hope spent most of her day sleeping, Sofia had made it a habit to force me out of the house every day. She said I was driving her crazy, sitting around staring at her all day long, but she didn't realize how mesmerized I was by both her and the baby we created.

I wanted to help, to do everything, but realized pretty early on that there wasn't much for me to do. Sofia breastfed our little angel and I changed her diapers—badly—whenever she let me, which honestly wasn't very often. I think she'd been so used to doing everything on her own that she forgot I was there to help. Or maybe she was tired of fixing all my diaper mishaps. It was probably a little of both.

Matson and I tried to come up with a plan to steal the baby one afternoon so Sofia could sleep all day and not worry, but we failed. Sofia yelled, so Matson and I left and played at the beach until dusk. After that, I started bringing him to the bar with me so we could both get out of the house together, and Sofia only had to tend to one kid instead of two. Even though it wasn't technically legal to have Matson in the bar during operating hours, it was worth the risk it posed if we got caught, especially if we were going to lose the bar anyway. What would it matter? We never stayed for very long, and Matson loved it there.

"When I grow up, can I work here?" he asked one afternoon, and my heart cracked in two inside my chest.

"Absolutely. I'll teach you everything I know," I said, hoping to God it wasn't a lie, and that the bar would still be standing when Matson was old enough to work here.

"Cool," he said as he spun on the bar stool.

"Are you going to make drinks like Ryan, or do you want to be a marketing genius like me?" Nick asked.

Matson put a finger on his chin as he pondered the question. "Probably both," he said with confidence. "I can do both, right?"

Nick grinned at him. "You can do anything you want."

When I grunted in frustration, Nick shook his head at me.

"How do you still not know how to do that?"

I glared at him, then stared down at the baby doll on top of the bar that I'd been practicing putting a diaper on. I lifted it into the air and watched as the diaper came undone and fell off. Nick and Matson both laughed.

"It's not as easy as it looks," I grumbled, dropping the dumb doll.

Nick waltzed over, grabbed the doll and the diaper, and within two seconds had it on perfectly. Why could everyone else and their dog put a diaper on a baby without any issues, and I couldn't?

"You can't be good at everything, brother," Nick said, laughing at my dejected expression.

"But I need to be good at this. I need to be able to put a diaper on my daughter and not have it fall off the second she starts wiggling."

"Mama said you're not allowed to anymore," Matson said, still spinning his bar stool.

My head swung in his direction. "What?"

He stopped spinning and looked up at me with wide eyes. "Uh, maybe I wasn't supposed to tell you that."

"It's okay," I said with a sigh. "She's right. But I'll figure it out."

I reached for the fake baby one more time and undid Nick's diaper. I was determined to get it right, and I wasn't going to stop until I did.

Reaching for my phone, I pulled up YouTube and searched for a tutorial. After watching it several times, I attempted the process again and let out a whoop of joy when I lifted the fake baby and the diaper stayed in place. I even shook the doll to see if the diaper would come undone, but it didn't.

"I did it! I finally fucking did it!"

"Uh, bad word." Matson stopped spinning and stared at me wide-eyed.

Crap. "Sorry, buddy. I just got really excited."

"I won't tell," he said, and went back to spinning.

ONE FISHER DOWN

Ryan

"**F**RAAANK!"

The sound of Jess's panicked voice froze the three of us brothers where we were waiting in the pastor's office for the wedding to start.

Nick reacted first, heading for the door at the same time that Jess burst through it. "What's the matter? What's wrong?" he asked as he reached for her.

She moved out of his grasp, clearly in a hurry. "Nothing, maybe. I just need to show Frank something and see if he freaks out."

I cast a quick glance at my older brother, who looked just as confused as the rest of us.

"Read this." She shoved a small notecard into his hands.

Nick and I huddled around Frank, trying to read it over his shoulder but failing. It looked like a welcome announcement of some kind from Frank and Claudia, and I assumed they were being handed out to the wedding guests upon their arrival this morning at the church.

"What am I looking for here, Jess?" He handed the notecard back to her, and she shook her head with a satisfied smile.

"I knew it. I knew you wouldn't even see it. Most people read things too fast, and their brain fixes the mistake instead of registering it."

"What mistake?" I took the paper and started laughing immediately. "Farnk? They spelled your name F-A-R-N-K! Oh, this is too much."

Nick ripped it from my grasp and cracked up. "Farnk Fisher."

"This isn't funny, assholes!" Jess told us, and we immediately tried to stop laughing. "Claudia's freaking out. She thinks Frank is going to be pissed."

Frank pushed back from his chair and stood to his full height, towering over Jess. "Jess, please go tell my fiancée that I'm not pissed, or upset, or anything else she's worried about. I couldn't care less about this stupid piece of paper."

He stopped short and held up a hand. "Maybe don't tell her that part. Just tell her I want to marry her, and that's all that matters."

Jess breathed out a sigh of relief. "I told her you wouldn't care, that guys don't give two shits about this kind of stuff, but she wasn't convinced."

"Go calm her down for me, please." He leaned over to give Jess a quick peck on the side of the head, and I swore I heard Nick growl. We Fishers are a possessive bunch.

"Okay. I'll see you guys in a bit." She turned to leave but then stopped and gave Nick a hard kiss. "You all look really fucking hot, by the way," she said, waving her hand at us in our formalwear, then rushed out the door the same way she'd come in.

"So, Farn—" I started to call Frank by his new nickname, and he took a menacing step toward me, shutting me up.

"Don't start. I told Jess I didn't care so that she'd calm Claudia down. But who the hell messes up the groom's name on a welcome card? The printers had one job to do. One!"

"It will be a funny memory?" Nick sounded so unconvinced, it came out like a question.

"I swear to God, I'll punch you both in the face if you start calling me that."

I scoffed. "You can't give us black eyes. It'll ruin your wedding pictures, Farnk."

Nick tried to hold back a laugh, but failed miserably. Frank clenched his hands into fists, and I raised my palms in surrender.

"Kidding. Kidding. I won't say it anymore." When his hands unclenched, I mumbled, "To your face."

"Let's have a drink." Nick raised one of the shot glasses I'd brought for us with a bottle of tequila, and set it on the table in a damn good distraction tactic.

"Great idea. Here. Drink this." I poured a shot of tequila in front of Frank and waited for him to pick up the glass. "It will help calm the nerves."

"I'm not nervous." He glared at me but took the drink anyway.

"I wouldn't be either," Nick lied, pouring himself a shot and downing it.

"Fine. None of us are nervous." I poured another round for us. "Drink up."

"Why are we drinking?" Frank growled as he adjusted his tie.

"It's what men do on their wedding day," I said as if I were an authority on the subject.

Nick nodded. "He's right. We're supposed to drink before we all walk down the aisle."

"No more," Frank said after swallowing his third shot. "I'd like to remember every single detail about this day."

I smiled inwardly. Two years ago, I would have sworn this day would never come. Before he met Claudia, Frank had been stuck in a relationship, bound by guilt and obligation. It had been no way to live, but he couldn't seem to see his way out of it.

I never thought I'd see a time when Frank wasn't with Shelby, but I also suspected he'd never walk down the aisle with her, no matter how much she had wanted it or how guilty he felt. It was only once Claudia was in the picture that Frank's entire demeanor changed. He came to life. He had hope again. And I hadn't realized just how hopeless he'd become until I had something to compare it to.

Now I couldn't imagine him with anyone else. Marrying Claudia wasn't an option for him, it was a necessity, like continuing with life without making her a Fisher would be all sorts of wrong. I understood it completely because it was how I felt about Sofia. And it was how Nick felt about Jess.

Our dad poked his head into the small room, then stepped inside. "You guys ready?"

"Hey, Dad," we all said in unison.

"It's a full house out there. How you feeling, son?" Smiling, he clapped a hand on Frank's shoulder.

"Great," Frank said.

Dad laughed. "Then get out there and get the girl."

"I plan on it."

Dad dropped his hand from Frank's shoulder, and his expression turned serious. "It was nice what you did. For Claudia's family."

"She really wanted them here. And they wanted to be here, especially after the proposal." Frank smiled, probably remembering his trip to Colombia with Claudia that he'd planned with the help of Claudia's mom and stepdad. It was where he'd proposed.

"Couldn't have been easy," Dad said.

Frank shook his head. "Oh, it wasn't. Immigration and visas are a total pain in the ass. I don't recommend trying it."

"Well, I'm glad it all worked out. You all look nice, by the way. Your mother and I are really proud. Of all three of you." His gaze roamed each of our faces. "You've done well for yourselves, both in life and love."

"Thanks, Dad," we chimed back.

I had to stop the emotion from welling up and coming out. Frank would never forgive me if I cried on his wedding day.

"One down, two to go," Dad said, pointing at me and Nick as he headed toward the door.

Frank sucked in a deep breath, and then gave us a huge grin. "Let's do this."

Nick and I both smiled back and reached for our tuxedo jackets. Standing by Frank's side while he married Claudia would be the easiest thing we'd do all day.

We walked down the hallway and then through the open doors toward the altar. Cream-colored flowers and gold candles adorned the sanctuary, setting an elegant romantic vibe. It was stunning, to say the least.

Yeah, I know. Dudes shouldn't love this kind of shit, but I did.

As we walked past my parents in the front row, who held my daughter and sat with my son, I gave Matson a quick wave. He grinned and waved back before looking down the aisle, most likely for his mother.

Since we brothers were all up front at the altar, our girls were walking down the aisle toward us alone. It was a little nontraditional, but Claudia had told us months ago that they didn't even do bridesmaids in Colombia, so the fact that she had any at all wasn't customary in her native country.

Watching Frank's face as he watched his bride walk down the aisle almost caused me to cry like the little girl he always accused me of being. But that was nothing compared to the way it felt to see Sofia standing there dressed in gold. That sight alone almost brought me to my knees. I couldn't help but imagine the two of us getting married, and I knew she felt it too.

She kept catching me watching her during the vows, and when the promises of forever were made, my eyes never left my woman's. Not even when her cheeks turned pink. Not even when Nick elbowed me in the ribs. I swore to myself that would be us someday soon.

As Frank and Claudia were pronounced Mr. and Mrs. Fisher, everyone in the church rose to their feet and cheered. I'd never seen my brother look so happy in my entire life. He leaned over to kiss Claudia one more time, and then they started their walk back down the aisle hand in hand, both wearing giant smiles.

The rest of us in the wedding party grinned at each other, eager to get the party started. Weddings were romantic as hell, but the reception was always the best part.

Frank and Claudia disappeared somewhere with the photographer. The rest of us in the wedding party filed into one of the rooms in the back, waiting for our cue to head out to the cars that waited to drive us to the reception.

"I couldn't take my eyes off you," I whispered into Sofia's ear as I brushed a strand of her hair off her shoulder.

She gave me a knowing grin. "I noticed."

"You liked it."

She shook her head. "I loved it."

"That's going to be us real soon." Pressing a kiss to her cheek, I lingered for a moment and breathed her in.

"Soon, huh?" She leaned back and gave me a look.

"You'll see," I promised.

"Stop whispering," Nick said as he pulled a flask from his jacket pocket and handed it to me.

"Tequila?" I asked.

"Bourbon."

I shrugged, then took a pull and handed it back to him.

Jess gave him a little shove. "You didn't even ask me if I wanted some."

"You don't like bourbon, babe," he said.

"But you could have at least asked," she said with a pout.

I glanced at Sofia, who was smiling at the pair. I felt a little bad that she couldn't drink because she was breastfeeding, but she told me it wasn't a big deal. Everyone tried to get her to "pump and dump," but she hadn't wanted to.

After she filled me in on exactly what the hell pump and dump even meant, I didn't argue. My angel knew what was best for her and the baby, and it was my job to support her decision. If she wanted to down tequila shots tonight, I'd happily go grab her a bottle. If she wanted to drink iced tea all evening long, then I'd refill her glass. Whatever she wanted, I was going to do it.

Done with the photographer, Frank and Claudia walked through the door, and we all moved to congratulate them at once, hugging, high-fiving, and doling out compliments.

"You ready to get out of here or what?" Claudia asked, her hand firmly grasped in Frank's.

"Hell yes," I answered for everyone.

"Let's go party!" She did a little shimmy move with her hips.

I gave Frank a look that told him he was in for some trouble, the best kind, and he gave me a nod that told me he knew.

The drive to the reception hall took less than five minutes. Once we all arrived and climbed out of the cars, we stood there in a haphazard group, waiting for directions from the photographer, who was still figuring out where exactly to start shooting first.

"You look so fucking beautiful, angel." I kissed Sofia's cheek as my mom joined us with baby Hope in her arms and Matson at her side.

"Thank you." Sofia gave me a sweet smile as she reached for Hope. "I should go feed her. Think I have time?"

"They can take other pictures while you do that. I'm sure it's fine." I gave her a quick kiss on the mouth and smacked her ass. "Go!"

Matson laughed, and I wrapped an arm around his shoulders.

"Thanks for watching them, Mom."

"Of course, honey. They're perfect." She mussed Matson's hair, and he smiled up at her. This was what happiness looked and felt like; I was sure of it.

After the most ridiculous number of pictures known to man had been taken, we finally headed into the reception hall. Claudia's Colombian touches were downright adorable. Each place card sat positioned inside a tray filled with coffee beans. It smelled amazing. And at each table were tiny satchels of Colombian coffee for guests to take home.

I kept picking mine up and sniffing at it. Matson mimicked me once and wrinkled his nose in distaste. "Ick," he said, tossing it onto the table.

I laughed. "One day you'll love it."

"Probably not."

The waitstaff wandered throughout the hall, filling everyone's glasses with champagne. When a gentleman I didn't know handed me a microphone, I knew it was time. With one look at Nick, I stood up from my chair at the head table and tapped the top of the microphone to get the room's attention.

"Hi, everyone. Not sure who this Farnk guy is," I

said, holding up one of the notecards from earlier, and the guests roared with laughter. Well, everyone except Frank laughed. I assumed he was plotting my death, based on the dark look he gave me.

"Sorry. That was the last time," I promised, giving him a shrug. "Like I was saying, I'm Frank's more charming, better-looking, younger brother Ryan."

Nick coughed and punched at his chest while the crowd laughed.

"And that's Nick." I hooked a thumb toward him. "He's less charming, but probably still better looking."

The crowd continued to laugh while Frank pretended to glare at me, shaking his head.

"Nick and I wrote this together because we knew we'd both say pretty much the same thing, but would spend the whole time trying to outdo each other. Instead of embarrassing Frank in front of everyone here today, we decided to combine our speeches and I'd deliver it. More charming, see?"

I made eye contact around the room and stopped on Claudia. "We're not sure what our brother was doing before he found you, Claudia, but it sure wasn't living. He hit the lottery the night you walked into our bar, and we all knew it. We saw the way he looked at you. And the way you looked back, if I'm being honest. If eye contact could start a fire, you two would have set the block ablaze, not just the bar. The whole damn block."

Overcome with emotion, I sucked in a breath. "You

saved him, you know. You brought the light back into his life, and we can never thank you enough for that. We can't imagine him with anyone else. You are our brother's perfect person. We're so grateful for you. And we're so excited to finally have a sister. Welcome to the Fisher family. We couldn't love you more."

I raised my glass of champagne, locking eyes with my brother and his new wife, who was wiping fresh tears away with a napkin. "To Frank and Claudia," I said, and everyone repeated the words as they toasted their neighbors and then took a sip.

As if on cue, the volume in the room immediately rose, with everyone speaking excitedly to each other. An army of waitstaff appeared, delivering the first course to each table at once.

"I need something stronger than this." I put down the champagne flute and looked at Sofia. "Do you want anything from the bar?" I knew she'd say no, but I wanted to ask anyway.

"I'm good, thanks."

"See, Nick?" Jess said, and I stifled a laugh, knowing what was coming. "Ryan knew Sof was gonna say no, but he asked her anyway."

"What can I say? I'm sorry I'm a shitty boyfriend," he said, pushing out his bottom lip in a pretend pout.

Jess reached for his cheeks and squeezed them with both hands. "You're not a shitty boyfriend." She kissed his face. "I love you. Just be more courteous sometimes, please?" she asked sweetly, and he grinned at her.

"I will, babe. Promise." Nick leaned over and kissed her hard.

"You coming?" I asked him.

He raised a glass half-filled with amber liquid in my direction, indicating that he was good.

Making my way toward the back bar, I stopped and shook hands with people I barely knew and accepted their compliments on my speech. I was thankful that most of the guests were busy eating, so the bar wasn't crowded. After ordering a drink, I dropped a tip in the jar and gave the bartender a nod when he sat my drink in front of me.

I noticed Grant making his way toward me, and so I stayed put, sipping my so-so drink. They're never as good as I make them.

He stopped in front of me, one hand in his jacket pocket. "Nice speech."

"Is that a compliment from you?"

"Eh." He shrugged. "I could have done better."

I laughed. "Not sure why you're always trying to compete with me."

"It's not competing when you always win," he bit back, and I rolled my eyes. "What, no snappy comeback? You're losing your touch."

For a second, I considered telling Grant about our problem with the bar. It certainly wasn't the right time, but a part of me longed to tell him. What if he could help somehow? I knew Frank would kill me if I spilled our dirty little secret on his wedding day, so I kept the information to myself.

"I'm not losing anything, old man. You've got your own angel now, right? Looks like we both win." I gave him a wink and gestured toward Mariana, who stood chatting with my mom.

"Is that your way of asking me a question, boy?" he said after he ordered two beers.

Everyone knew Grant and Mariana had been inseparable since they'd met, but nobody ever said anything to their faces. Instead, we all commented on it and tried to figure out their situation behind their backs.

"Fine. Are you two dating? Together? What is it that old people do?"

He cast me a look I couldn't quite read as he took a long swig of his beer. "I'll only say this once, so listen up. My wife was the love of my life. The love of my life," he repeated. "And I know that she wouldn't want me to get remarried. She was a jealous old bat, and she'd turn over in her grave if I even thought about it. But she would have wanted me to be happy and have good company. That's what I've found with Mariana, and I believe that's what she's found with me. It's better than being alone, I'll tell you that much."

"How do you even get her to want to spend time with you? Are you actually nice to her?" I teased, knowing I was poking the bear.

Grant harrumphed. "I'm charming, and you know it.

It's why you look up to me. One day, maybe you'll learn a thing or two from the master."

I pretended to choke on my drink. "The master? The second you start teaching classes, I'll be the first to sign up."

"You'd be wise to," he said as he walked away, a beer in each hand.

The old man was crazy, but he was right. I did sort of look up to him, and he knew it.

ELEPHANT IN THE ROOM

Ryan

AFTER I'D POURED three beers and made five cocktails, the bar patrons seemed content.

Frank worked beside me, finishing making drinks for a couple of girls. He hadn't spent more than five minutes in the office these past few weeks. He'd been on the floor, making drinks, closing tabs, and helping out like he did when we first took over the business.

Nick wiped his hands on a towel as he made his way to the end of the bar, away from customers and prying ears. Frank and I followed his lead, knowing we needed to talk about the elephant in the room.

Personally, I was glad that Frank's wedding was over. It wasn't that I wasn't happy for my brother, but we needed to focus on the bar situation, and the wedding had been a distraction. A great distraction, of course, but a distraction nonetheless.

Frank twisted the wedding ring on his finger, and I wondered if I'd ever get used to seeing it there.

"Does it bug you?" I asked.

He glanced down at his left hand. "Nah, I'm just not

used to anything on my finger. And it's heavy."

"I bet it wouldn't be too heavy for Farnk."

I grinned at him, unable to help myself. The mistake with his name was way too fucking golden to let go and never bring up again. So far, he hadn't noticed the one welcome card that I'd tacked up on the wall of the office. Or maybe he had? I hadn't been in there yet today.

"Joke's old," he said, trying to sound threatening, but I wasn't biting.

"It just started," I said. "It can't be old already."

"Are you two done?" Nick asked, and we both shot him a murderous glare. "We have shit to talk about."

"You're right," I said, putting on my serious face.

Nick glanced at Frank. "I'm really glad you're not on your honeymoon right now."

I couldn't have agreed more. I'd given Frank so much shit over it initially, telling him it was tradition to leave right away. But now, I thanked God that Claudia's family decided to stay in town longer and extend their vacation, so Frank and Claudia had delayed their honeymoon.

"I wouldn't have been able to enjoy myself, and Claudia would have killed me for ruining our honeymoon." Frank ran a hand through his dark hair. "She still doesn't know this is even going on."

"Jess doesn't either."

I shook my head. "I haven't said a word to Sofia."

The door opened, and three women walked in wearing too-white smiles that widened when they caught sight of the three of us in the corner. They looked almost identical with their bleached-blond hair, unnatural tans, and matching outfits.

The triplets made their way toward us, despite my silent pleas begging them to stay away. My brothers and I still needed to talk, and unless we went into the office, we couldn't have any privacy. And there was no way we were leaving the bar unattended.

The women sat down and grabbed three menus from the bar top, perusing them.

"I'll be with you ladies in a minute." I gave them a smile and they all nodded so fast, I thought their heads might fall off their shoulders.

I turned toward Frank and Nick again, tightening our huddle and keeping our voices low. "We need to figure out what the hell is going on with that deed. Still no word from the courthouse on any updated ownership?" I looked at Frank, and he shook his head.

"No, but our lawyer says that we can slow down the takeover with a bunch of legalities, considering we truly thought we were purchasing the land and we've been paying taxes on it. But that's all it most likely would be. A stall to buy us more time."

"More time would be good," Nick said, his voice hopeful. "I don't understand how we don't have any rights if Sam thought he sold us the land, we had a land deed authorized, and we've been paying taxes on it. How do we not have a case?"

I nodded. "He makes a good point."

"There's a chance we could fight this, but it might ending up taking a really long time. We'd probably have to close the bar while we were in litigation, and winning isn't a guarantee," Frank said, sounding defeated.

"More time would be good," I said. "But I guess not if the bar had to be closed."

"And if we're probably going to lose out in the end, what difference does more time make?" Frank held up a hand as both Nick and I opened our mouths to argue the point. "I'm just being realistic. It's going to buy us more time to do what? If we have to leave Sam's and open a new bar somewhere, we're going to have to do that anyway. Why wait? Why waste any more time than we have to?"

My annoyance dwindled immediately. Frank made a fair point. I had no idea what the right thing to do was. "What did the sale paperwork say exactly?"

"It says we own the bar and the back lot in part one of two sales. Part two was the land purchase. It states that the deed filed is not the original, even though it's been notarized. It wasn't uncommon for paperwork to go missing from that time period. We did everything by the book, but it doesn't matter, not if there's an original signed deed out there."

"We're going to actually read this thing, right? I mean, that guy wouldn't even let me touch it. What if it's not real?"

"Fuck yes, we're reading it." Frank gave me an exasperated look. "We're not walking away from our business without solid proof."

I raised my hands in the air in surrender. "Just making sure."

"Come on, Ryan. We're not just taking some asshole's word for it and handing over the keys."

"I'm just saying . . . I know we've all talked about stepping away from the bar more—"

Nick interrupted me. "We just said that we wanted to stop working every night shift, not lose the bar altogether."

He was right. I was being emotional. The three of us had talked at length about our futures, what we wanted going forward, and what that meant realistically for the business. We all wanted our own families and lives outside of work, but we also wanted to keep the bar.

"And we've already started to do that," Frank said. "We're here in the days mostly now, and we hired Max to manage the night shifts. It's been great."

"Plus, there's that second location we've always talked about opening," I said, feeling that prickle of excitement whenever we talked about growing the business.

It was something we talked about all the time in the beginning, but our vision changed as our success grew and we met the girls. None of us wanted to have to physically be at each location we opened for it to succeed. At this point, we figured that our name alone would make the business a success, but even that assumption came with risks.

"Let's worry about this location first before we even contemplate another," Frank said, bringing me back to reality.

"Excuse me." The woman's voice cut through our pow-wow, and we all turned at the same time. "We know what we want." She placed the menus down and pushed them away.

I pasted on a smile and approached the smiling group. "Are you sisters?"

They giggled. "No, but we get that a lot."

"You look a lot alike," I said, somewhat fascinated by their almost identical features.

"We have the same plastic surgeon," Triplet Number Two said, and I stopped myself from asking any more questions I truly didn't care about the answers to.

"All right. Well, what can I get you ladies?"

"Can we get three Happy Endings?"

I couldn't help but smile at their drink choice. It was my newest creation, and I knew they'd love it. Everyone who had tried it so far couldn't stop at one.

Triplet Number Three spoke for the first time since they'd come in. "Is it really purple? I mean, it says purple gin on the menu, but is the gin purple or is that just the name?"

"It's really purple. You'll love it." I gave them a wink and turned to grab the ingredients.

After mixing purple gin with fresh-squeezed lime juice and soda, I swirled each glass and then garnished it with a small flower. When I handed them their drinks, they all oohed and aahed at how pretty they were, and then pulled out their phones to take pictures to post on social media.

The cell phone shit used to annoy me, but Nick changed my way of thinking. Encouraging posts on social media that tagged our bar was good for business, helping to get the word out whenever we created something new. It was free publicity, easy and effortless.

I stood in front of the girls until they tried their drinks, wanting to see their reactions. After they sipped, their eyes met mine.

"Good?" I asked, even though I knew how good the cocktail was.

"It's delicious." Triplet Number Three hummed her appreciation and took another sip.

"So light and refreshing," Triplet Number One added.

"I didn't even know I liked gin," Number Three said, and I laughed. I'd heard that more than a handful of times since I started making this particular drink.

"I'll start a tab for you ladies." I picked up the credit card one of them had placed on top of the bar and tucked it in a glass near the register.

Business picked up, which meant our ability to talk privately was pretty much over for the night. I noticed

Frank still standing in the same place where I'd left him. I wandered over, about to give him shit for not doing something useful, when Nick joined us.

"So, I was thinking," Nick said, then stopped short. His brow furrowed like he was deep in thought as Frank and I waited for him to continue. "If we're going to lose this location, I kind of want to do something special for Jess here."

"What do you mean?" I asked.

"I want to propose."

Nick's smile took up his whole damn face, and I couldn't even give him shit for it. He'd had Jess's ring sitting in the bar safe for almost as long as he'd been working here.

"Here? In the bar?" Frank asked. We used to tease Nick about actually putting the damn thing on her finger, but neither of us ever contemplated that he'd choose the bar as his setting to do it.

"Hell yes, here. It's where I brought her after formal. It's where I came to talk to you guys when I almost lost her forever. It's where we both came back to. This bar holds a lot of memories for us, and I'd like it to hold one more."

Nick was adamant. He couldn't be talked out of this idea, not that I planned on trying.

"Okay, when?" I asked.

"The day before the deadline."

Frank coughed and slapped his chest. "That's in five

days. Seriously? Of all the days, you want to do it then?"

"What difference does it make? Plus, it's Jess's birthday." Nick shrugged, and we had nothing to say back. Truthfully, it made no difference.

"We're in." Frank gave our youngest brother a small grin, and I slapped him on the back in congratulations.

"Excuse me?" the triplets sang out in unison. "Can we get three more Happy Endings?"

I turned toward them, surprised they'd polished off their first round so quickly. A few more of those at that rate, and the girls would need to be carried out.

I went to work making the drink that I'd created with my brothers and me in mind. It was supposed to represent the love that we'd found and the happiness we had in our lives. But I was starting to worry that maybe I'd inadvertently made a drink that represented the end of our bar and our life as we knew it.

A Happy *Ending* indeed. Maybe I should have named it Happy Days instead.

ONE LAST SURPRISE

Ryan

I TAPED THE laser-printed sign to the front door of Sam's that said we were closed for a private event and would reopen to the public at eight p.m. Hoping it wouldn't blow away with the ocean breeze, I slapped on one more piece of adhesive, just to be sure.

In less than twenty-four hours, we would potentially lose the bar and everything we'd worked so hard to create. I knew the three of us were thinking the exact same thing, but we did our best to hide it.

Today was a celebration, and Nick had been right. If we were going to walk away from this place, we might as well have one last amazing memory made inside these walls.

Nick had invited all of our families and a handful of our friends here for Jess's birthday celebration. He left out the majority of her coworkers, telling us that there was a difference between Jess's friends in the office and her real-life ones. It made perfect sense to me, but as usual, Frank complained. I think he just wanted something to take his frustrations out on because his argument had been less than logical.

"Door locked?" Frank asked a few moments later as he joined me behind the bar.

"Yep." I looked over and watched as Nick wrapped an arm around Jess and pulled her in for a kiss.

I'd never seen them fight, which was saying a lot because of their age. Younger couples tended to argue over stupid shit, petty jealousy and whatnot, but not those two. It seemed like what they went through in their past was enough for both of them to stay appreciative and respectful of one another. They were so completely comfortable in each other's presence, it put everyone else at ease. That's how solid they were.

"We have a lot of family now," Frank said, giving me a meaningful look.

I surveyed the room again, this time paying more attention. It was filled with mostly extended family . . . from Sofia and Claudia's parents to Grant and Mariana. Our small Fisher clan had grown exponentially once we added the girls to it. It felt good. Right.

"I like it."

"Me too." He clapped a hand on my shoulder.

I searched for Sofia, spotting her off to the side in a yellow sundress that hugged her perfect curves, holding Hope. Matson, as usual, was practically glued to Jess's side. You had to hand it to the kid; he was loyal. He had drawn Jess a birthday picture earlier that he was excited to give her. I couldn't wait to see Nick's face when he realized that the prince in the picture was Matson, and the dragon had Nick's features. I laughed softly just thinking about it.

"Why do you have to ruin every moment by turning into such a girl?" Frank groaned. "What are you even laughing at, anyway?"

I rolled my eyes, which I knew would only irritate him more. "You'll see later. Go annoy your wife, and let me make everyone some drinks."

When he begrudgingly left me alone, I went to work making a tray full of Happy Endings and a few No Bad Days. Slipping out from behind the bar, I made my way through the crowd to distribute the drinks.

Claudia's best friend, Britney, stopped me first. "What's the purple one?"

"It's gin, soda, and lime. You'll like it."

"What's it called?" She grinned at me as she reached for a glass.

"Happy Ending."

"Well, isn't that just fitting," she teased.

I played dumb. "How do you mean?"

"I never thought you'd top Adios Pantalones, but then you go and name your next creation Happy Ending? You little perv."

"It's not my fault your mind's always in the gutter, Brit."

"I bet I'm not the only one." She smirked and took a sip. "Crap. This is good."

Grinning, I moved through our family and friends, tapping them on the shoulder to offer up drinks. I reached Rachel, Jess's best friend, with only one cocktail left on my tray.

"I wanted one of the purple ones," she said with a whine.

"I'll go make you one," I said, and her face instantly broke out into a huge smile.

"Thank you. But in the meantime, I'll take this while I'm waiting."

Britney reached for the last No Bad Days and took a giant gulp like it was filled with juice instead of premium vodka. I started to warn her to slow down, or maybe not to mix liquors, but stopped myself.

"It's adorable the way Matson loves Jess." She motioned toward him, and my gaze followed. He was still glued to Jess's side, and she had her arm wrapped around his shoulders.

"He's been obsessed with her since the minute he first saw her."

"Must run in the family." Britney nudged my body with her hip, and my heart swelled at her words. I often forgot that Matson wasn't my flesh and blood. It was nice hearing that someone else did too.

"I'll be back with your drink, slave driver," I teased, then headed toward my beautiful angel.

"Hi, baby," Sofia said as I bent down to give her a long-overdue kiss.

"How are my two angels doing?" I placed a gentle kiss on top of Hope's head.

I'd been concerned at first that Hope barely had any hair, and but Sofia acted like it was totally normal. It took a few days, but she finally convinced me that the baby's hair would eventually grow in and she wouldn't be bald forever.

"We're good," Sofia said as she swayed back and forth, rocking Hope.

"I have to go make some more drinks. You don't want anything, do you?"

She shook her head, and then her eyes widened. "Wait! Can I get a Diet Coke?"

"You can get anything you want."

Her voice turned playful. "Well, in that case . . ."

I cocked a brow in her direction, baiting her to finish that sentence. When she didn't, I sighed and headed back to the bar to mix a few more drinks.

After filling the tray four more times, I decided to take a break. As I was behind the bar washing some of the glasses we'd used tonight, Nick gestured for me to meet him in the back room, where the cake was waiting in a small refrigerator.

"What's up?" I dried my hands and tucked the towel into my back pocket where it seemed to live during shifts.

He blew out a long, dramatic breath. "This is it."

"Nervous?" I asked as he spun the combination lock on the safe and pulled down the handle.

The sound of the lock disengaging echoed in the small room, and the door creaked open as he reached inside. After pulling out the black ring box, he flipped it open, making sure the pear-shaped diamond still sat inside. It did. Of course it did. It had been sitting there for forever.

"I'm excited more than anything, but yeah, I'm a little nervous." Nick smiled at the ring, then closed the box and tucked it into his pocket. "What was I thinking, planning to propose in front of everyone we know?"

I shook my head, debating whether I should answer him honestly or give him some brotherly advice. "You were thinking that you wanted to make one last good memory here. And you wanted to do it in front of everyone who cares about you and Jess. This is a good thing, Nick. It's going to be amazing."

He nodded, his gaze bouncing everywhere but meeting mine. "Yeah. You're right. Okay." He turned to walk out of the room, but I stopped him.

"Bro, the cake."

"Shit." He stopped and turned back toward the fridge, and I laughed. I'd never seen him so flustered. It was amusing.

"You good?" I asked, and he nodded.

I left him unsupervised, deciding that if he didn't emerge from the office in less than five minutes, I'd go back in and get him. But Nick walked out a moment later, the cake topped with unlit candles in his hands.

I jogged into the office to be sure he hadn't taken the ring out of his pocket and left it behind. It would ruin his whole plan if he had. Scanning the room and finding no ring box in sight, I hustled back out into the bar, not wanting to miss a moment.

Finding Sofia, I wrapped my arm around her and pulled her against me. "I love you."

"I love you too." She snuggled into me as I reached for my cell phone and aimed it toward Nick and Jess, zooming the camera in closer.

"What are you doing?" she asked, looking confused.

"Just pay attention," I whispered, and her mouth dropped open.

"Is he? Oh my gosh, Ryan, is he going to propose? How could you keep this from me?" Her voice rose, and as a few people turned to look at us, I gave her a look that begged her to be quiet.

"Nick will kill me if we ruin this," I whispered to her. "Just watch."

I focused my attention and my camera phone back on Nick as the final candle on the cake was lit. Our parents stood next to Jess's, fully aware of what was about to happen.

Nick had asked Jess's dad for permission to marry his daughter over a year ago, but recently asked him again to make sure he hadn't changed his mind. Jess's dad had pretended like he wasn't sure, and Nick told me later how he'd freaked out and wondered what the hell he'd do if her dad didn't give his blessing again. Thankfully, he said yes, but warned Nick to hurry up already, because none of us were getting any younger.

After an off-key rendition of "Happy Birthday" was sung by everyone in the bar, Nick held up a hand for everyone to be quiet. Turning to Jess, he said, "Close your eyes and make a wish. It won't come true if you don't close your eyes first."

Jess smiled up at him and did what he asked.

The moment her eyes closed, my little brother pulled the ring box from his pocket and dropped to one knee. Sofia gasped softly next to me, but I refused to look at her, terrified I'd mess up the filming. Nick would never forgive me if my video turned into shots of Sofia's feet instead of his proposal.

Jess's eyes opened as she leaned over to blow out the candles, but she must have caught sight of Nick. Instead of blowing them out, she gasped with surprise.

"You made me ruin my wish," she choked out, her voice tight with emotion.

Laughter erupted as Nick said, "By all means, babe, blow them out first. I'll just wait here."

More laughter as Nick stayed on bended knee, and Jess blew out the candles quicker than I'd ever seen anyone do it.

As the room quieted, she focused her attention back on him. "What are you doing?"

"I let you go once," Nick said, "and it was the biggest

mistake of my life. I knew it then, and I know it now. I'll never forget what not having you in my life felt like. I never want to know that feeling again. And if you'll do me the honor of marrying me and becoming my wife, I'll never have to. I love you more than anything, Jess. Say yes. Say you'll be mine for the rest of time."

She nodded, tears streaming down her face, and he stood. She threw herself into Nick's arms and buried her head in his shoulder, then answered his question between peppering kisses all over his face.

"Yes. Of course yes. Always yes."

"Yes?" he asked, as if he wasn't sure he'd heard her correctly.

"Yes!" she shouted.

Nick released her and slid the ring on her finger, then she attacked him with kisses again.

Everyone in the room dabbed at their eyes, wiping away happy tears. Frank and Claudia were wrapped in each other's arms, and I pulled Sofia to my side so tightly, I thought she might complain, but she didn't.

I stopped recording and faced her. "How do you think Matson is going to take this news?"

She pondered the question, spotting her son as he made his way toward us. "I guess we're about to find out."

"Hey, buddy," I said as he walked over and stood between us. "Are you okay?"

"I'm happy they're getting married, but . . ." Matson

stopped and took in a deep breath, then let it out in an exaggerated sigh.

"But what?" Sofia asked.

I reached for Hope so she could give her attention to our boy. Tucking Hope into my arms, I started rocking the same way Sofia always seemed to do without thinking.

"Does that mean I can't ever marry Jess?"

Matson was so serious, it almost broke my heart, and Sofia looked up at me for help.

"You're going to find your own girl to marry someday," I said, but it seemed like little consolation.

"I don't want to find another girl." His expression clouded as he folded his arms and stared at the floor.

Sofia reached for his chin and tipped it up, then pulled him into a hug. "I know you don't. But one day you will. Jess will always be your favorite aunt. Okay?"

"I guess," he said sadly as he wriggled out of her arms.

I wanted to help, but wasn't sure how. "You like Nick, right?"

"Not right now," he answered honestly, and I couldn't help but laugh.

"Okay, well, you usually like Nick, don't you?"

He nodded and shrugged his shoulders simultaneously, still looking down.

"And you want your uncle Nick to be happy, right?"

Matson stayed quiet, and just when I thought he wasn't going to answer, a small *yeah* came out.

"Jess makes Nick happy," I said gently, trying to explain, but afraid I was totally blowing it.

"She makes me happy too. So maybe we can both marry her?"

Matson's face lit up like a Christmas tree, and before either Sofia or I could stop him, he turned and ran off, headed straight for Nick and Jess.

Sofia looked at me with a worried expression. "I should probably take him home and put Hope to bed." She reached for the baby and took her gently from my arms.

"I need to clean up and stay for a little while longer. You sure you want to leave without me?"

"I never want to leave without you, Ryan. But I'm exhausted."

I pulled her close and kissed her as passionately as I could with our baby girl between us. "I'll see you at home. I love you."

"I love you too." She rose up on tiptoe to kiss me again, then blew out a long breath. "Here goes nothing."

She headed toward Matson, who was animatedly discussing something with Nick. I could only imagine what was coming out of that kid's mouth.

EAVESDROPPING OLD MAN

Ryan

ONCE WE'D CLOSED the bar and only a few friends and family were left, I gathered up the last of the cocktail glasses. As I was washing them in the sink behind the bar, both Frank and Nick joined me to help dry and hang them up.

"Uh, thanks for whatever that was with Matson, bro," Nick said, and I pretended like I had no idea what he was talking about.

"Huh?"

"The kid is in love with my girl. He said that the only fair thing is if we share her. We both get to marry her, and she lives with each of us off and on throughout the week," Nick explained, and I burst out laughing.

"At least he had a plan," Frank said, sounding impressed. "Nice proposal, by the way. You did good."

"Thanks. And thanks for getting the whole thing on video, Ryan."

"Of course. She was surprised, yeah? Didn't see it coming?"

A wicked grin crept across Nick's face. "She had no

idea."

"That's the best," I said as I kept washing. Glancing at the clock on the wall, I realized we had a little over forty minutes until we reopened to the public.

"Think he'll show up tomorrow?" Nick reached for a clean glass from my hand and started drying it.

"He'll definitely show up. Unless he died," Frank said with a shrug.

"Think he'll come alone again?" Nick asked, and I realized that it hadn't even occurred to me that he might come with backup.

Nerves tied my stomach in knots. "Do we have a plan? What if he shows up with the whole damn mob or something." I had no idea what the hell we were going to do when the guy stormed back into our bar and demanded the keys to it.

Grant's sarcastic voice broke through our otherwise hushed tones. "What are you girls carrying on about back here?"

"Nothing," I said, hoping that would be the end of it. But this was Grant we were talking about.

He pounded a fist on the bar top, drawing unwanted attention toward us. "Boys. Get over here right now and tell me what you're talking about. I might be able to help."

I exchanged glances with my brothers. Nick's eyes widened a little and Frank shrugged, so we wandered over to where Grant stood, his expression almost murderous.

Frank nodded at me to speak for us.

"Some scary-ass guy came in here," I told Grant, "saying that he owns the land the bar's sitting on. He wants to close it and tear it down."

Grant stayed silent for a beat, working his jaw. "What's this fellow look like?"

"Scary," Nick and I said in unison.

"Like mob scary?" Grant asked.

I cocked my head to the side. "What do you know about it, old man?"

"Well, I'll be damned." Grant shook his head as a sly smile formed. It was the last thing I expected to see at a stressful time like this.

"Why are you smiling?" Frank asked, sounding as irritated as I felt.

"Because I know what the fella wants."

When Grant didn't say anything more, I nearly lost my temper. "Are you going to tell us what that is?" If I had to drag the information out of him by force, I would.

He put an aged hand in the air and looked down, that stupid smile still on his face. "In a second. I just can't believe everything that old geezer said was true."

The three of us stood there staring at him, our hearts in our throats as we waited impatiently for him to explain.

"If you're not going to help," Frank huffed, "I don't have time for this." He turned to go.

"Wait a damn minute," Grant shouted, and a sliver of

shock coursed through me as Frank complied.

Grant looked behind his shoulder to make sure no one else could hear, then waved us closer. "I used to come here a lot. Got to know Sam Jr. pretty well, long before you boys bought the place. He used to tell me all kinds of stories, but that's what I always thought they were . . . stories that he made up. They sounded so farfetched, but I guess they weren't."

"I need you to start making sense, Grant, because you're not making any," Nick said, clearly as anxious as the rest of us.

The old man glanced over both shoulders again, seeming nervous. "He told me that an old mob boss had asked his father to hold some things for him back in the day. The mobster said he wasn't sure when he'd come back to collect the items, but that they'd better be waiting for him when he did. Sam Sr. knew the guy was serious, so he hid the stuff for him. And Sam Jr. told me they were still right where his dad left them all those years ago. He was terrified to move them. Told me he only even looked at them once, then never looked again."

"He didn't tell you what the guy gave him?" I asked.

Grant shook his head. "He had no idea. He said his dad put it away and they pretended that it never existed. Only talked about it once or twice. I reckon whatever that guy gave Sam's father is what your guy is after."

"Wait." Frank held a finger in the air to stop all con-versation, like this was something too insane to be true.

"Why would the mob be in Santa Monica? And why would he ask Sam's father to hold something for him? It makes no sense." Frank looked about as unconvinced as I was.

An annoyed grunt came from Grant. "Do you not know anything about Santa Monica's history? The mob used to come here all the time. It was their getaway spot before they turned their sights on Vegas. They hung out a lot at the Georgian Hotel right down the street. There was a speakeasy in the basement that they used during Prohibition. Apparently, this particular guy knew better than to try to keep whatever he wanted hidden there. He told Sam that the Georgian was too obvious a choice, it would be found in a heartbeat, but that no one would suspect Sam's Bar. He said they'd never even think to look for it here."

"Until now," I said with a huff.

"Until now." Grant nodded. "But this is the first time anyone's come looking, as far as I know. I didn't believe Sam when he told me, so I didn't ask a lot of questions."

"Do you know where it's hidden?" Frank's suspicious expression was gone. I knew he now believed everything Grant was telling us.

Grant's smile grew even wider, if that was possible. "I do."

"The hell, old man? Get up and show us." I glared at him, giving him a moment to move his ass before I hopped over the bar and moved it for him. Our livelihood was on the line, and I was tired of playing games.

"Do you have a safe in the office?" Grant asked, as if he didn't know the answer.

A full-sized safe was in the back office when we bought the bar. It was way too big and we didn't need it, but it weighed a million pounds, so we figured it was easier to keep it than to try to get rid of it or move it. Plus, it was cool as fuck to look at, and we liked it.

We filed into the office and stared at the safe like it was a brand-new addition instead of something that had been sitting here since the bar originally opened.

"Well, don't just stand there," Grant barked. "One of you dummies open it."

Frank shot him an annoyed look and then spun the combination lock. He pushed the large lever down, and with a loud click that echoed in the small room, the safe door swung open. "Now what?"

We stared into the darkness, the three of us all too familiar with what lay inside. It was mostly empty at the moment, just a few important papers, some extra cash, and small boxes. We locked up the cash from the till, the credit card machine, and our business laptops inside the safe after closing each night, but that was about it.

"Sam said there was a false back." Grant pointed toward the rear of the safe, where you couldn't really see anything in the darkness.

"A false back?" Nick asked. "Like a fake panel that can be moved?"

I glanced around the office, convinced we were being punked. There was no way in hell this craziness was real. But then I thought about all the things we'd been through as a family, and realized that this was no more farfetched than the rest of our lives had been so far.

"Get in there, Nick, and check," I demanded, and he narrowed his eyes at me.

"Why do I have to go in? You go in," he shot back.

Frank and I both yelled at him in unison, "Get in."

Nick groaned but did as we asked. As he crouched into the safe between the shelving, I shined the flashlight from my cell phone into the darkness. He inspected the back wall, feeling along its edges.

"Shit," he said, and we all craned our necks to see what he was looking at. "This moves, I think."

With a click and a small crash, Nick turned around to face us, a black steel panel in his hands. I shined my light around his shoulders and noticed a hole chiseled in the brick wall behind the safe. It looked like something out of a prison movie, where they started to try to dig their way out.

"Holy shit," I whispered as Nick put the panel on the floor and snatched my phone from my hand so he could see in the hole.

"That old son of a gun," Grant said, grinning. "He wasn't lying."

"Is there anything in there?" Frank asked.

"Yeah," Nick said. "There is."

He shined the light into the makeshift hole as he reached into it, his arm almost all the way in to his shoulder. When he pulled it back out, he held three dust-covered cloth bags.

"Hold on, there's something else back there." He handed us the bags and shoved his arm back in the hole again.

Frank and I dropped the old bags on top of the desk and focused our attention back on Nick. His entire arm was inside that hole as he struggled to reach whatever it was that only he could see, his body wiggling and stretching. When he pulled back out, he had a faded piece of paper in his grasp.

We huddled close, struggling to all read it at the same time.

"It's a deed," Nick said, his brow furrowed as Frank asked to see it.

"It's the deed to this land." Frank sounded shocked as my confusion kicked into full gear.

"But that man had the deed," I said, remembering that I'd clearly seen the word *deed* on the paper he showed me, but refused to let me touch. "Unless it wasn't the deed for here. Or even a real deed at all."

"I'm sure it wasn't. The mob doesn't usually play by the rules," Grant said. "They'd lie, manipulate, and murder to get what they want."

"So we have the deed to the land then?" I asked again, stunned. "And that guy doesn't."

"We have it. But I bet he wants whatever's in these bags." Nick gestured toward them, then grabbed the plate and secured it in the back of the safe again.

Frank reached for one of the old twine ties around one sack and gave it a tug. The fabric was brittle with age, and flakes of it dropped off as it practically fell apart in his hands.

"Go slow," the rest of us cried out.

Frank glared at us. "I'm not an idiot."

Opening the bag, he spread the top part wide so we could see inside. I peered in, finding exactly what I'd expected to see inside—stacks of cash money and mounds of jewelry. I had no idea how much money was there. The bills were old and looked almost fake, unlike any dollars I'd ever seen.

"We've got to call the police," Nick said, wiping his dusty hands on his jeans and leaving dirty handprints on them.

"What are you guys doing back here?" Jess, Claudia, and our mother stood in the office doorway, staring at us curiously. "We've been looking all over for you."

"And that's my cue," Grant said as he moved to leave the room. "I'll go make that phone call." He moved past the women and closed the door behind him.

"What's going on?" Mom asked.

They knew we were keeping something from them, so we asked them to sit down while we explained everything. Our mom and Claudia took the office chairs while Jess perched on the edge of the desk, their eyes widening as our story unfolded.

"I can't believe you guys didn't tell us," Claudia said when we'd finished. She narrowed her eyes on the three of us, and then her disappointed gaze landed squarely on Frank.

"And we could have helped," Mom added. "Your father and I can always help."

When Frank shrugged, looking uncomfortable, I stepped in. "That's just it, Mom. You couldn't help. Not with this. We called our lawyer, and he's been working on it, but there's only so much he could do. We could barely even talk about it with each other, let alone anyone else."

Frank spread his hands wide. "We never want to let you down, and we didn't know what was going to happen. Until we knew for sure, we just kept it between us three."

Even as he said the words, I knew it wouldn't be enough. There was no reason good enough to keep something this big from the people we loved.

"You can't do that," Jess said, clearly irritated. "You don't get to pick and choose what to tell us and what to leave us out of."

"Yeah. We're your teammates, right? Your partners?" Claudia asked, her eyes piercing Frank's, making me thankful that Sofia had already gone home for the night. "Then you share everything with us. Even the hard stuff."

"Especially the hard stuff," Jess added, her voice firm.

"We have a right to know what's going on."

"When was this deadline?" Mom asked.

I swallowed hard. "Tomorrow."

"Tomorrow?" the three of them practically shouted in unison. They jumped up from their seats, becoming more riled up by the second.

"I can't believe you kept this from us." Claudia paced angrily back and forth in the small space. "I'm so mad at you! And you." She shot me a look that made me want to crawl into the safe and hide. "Sofia is going to kill you."

"I'm aware," I managed to say.

"You just proposed to me, you jackass!" Jess stepped toward Nick and poked him in the chest. "This isn't what we do. We don't keep things from each other."

"You're right. I'm sorry, babe. It won't happen again," he said sincerely, and she poked him again, still pissed.

The three of us tucked our proverbial tails between our legs and apologized. After we all promised to never keep something like that from them again, their anger seemed to fade.

A knock on the office door interrupted us, and Grant poked his head in. "The police are here."

"Already?" I asked.

"Must be a slow night." He held the door open, revealing two cops standing in the hallway.

The office was too small to hold everyone, so Frank asked the ladies to step outside with Grant as we ushered the cops in and closed the door behind us. The three of us explained to the policemen what we knew and answered all their questions while one of them took notes, writing down everything we said.

It took less than twenty minutes for them to hear our story, then walk out of the bar with the three bags of valuables and the original deed.

But not before we copied it first. I tried to get them to let us keep the original, but they said it had to be entered into evidence. I made five photocopies of the deed, just in case I lost the first four.

"What? I'm a little paranoid. Sue me," I said when Nick gave me shit as I copied it more than once.

"We're pretty sure you can have this back." One of the cops held up the deed once I was done with it. "Just give us twenty-four hours to process it. Then you can file a request to get it back."

"Will you find out where the money and jewelry came from?" Frank asked.

The cop shrugged. "We'll do our best, but no guarantees. Anything we find out that we can share, we'll let you know."

"Sounds good." Frank gave them each a firm handshake and moved to see them out.

Alone with Nick, I turned to face him, the weight on my shoulders I hadn't even realized I was carrying suddenly lifted. Inhaling deeply for what felt like the first time in weeks, I felt so light. I wanted to jump around and high-five everyone in the bar.

"I guess we get to make more memories here after all?" The smile on my face wasn't going away anytime soon.

"Hell yes, we are! I'm so relieved, Ryan," Nick said, and I pulled him into a brotherly hug.

"Me too. Me fucking too."

"And I'm engaged!" He gave me a shit-eating grin.

"That you are, little brother."

"I'm going to go find my fiancée and make sure she doesn't want to kill me." He gave me a sly nod and moved toward the door. "You gonna call Sofia and fill her in?"

"I probably should, huh?" It wasn't really a question.

"I'd tell her before one of the girls does."

He was right, but I waved him off. "Go. Enjoy being engaged. I've got this handled."

MOB HEISTS

Ryan

THE NEXT DAY, the three of us waited all afternoon for the guy who threatened our livelihood to walk through the door. We knew he could arrive at any moment, and that moment couldn't come soon enough.

My stomach twisted in anticipation and dread. Even though I knew we held all the cards, I had no idea what a man like that was capable of. I couldn't imagine him simply accepting the news. No, a guy with ties to the mob would most likely refuse to walk away emptyhanded.

"Did you tell Sofia everything?" Frank asked in a hushed tone as we continued to stare at the door.

"Yeah, I told her last night."

"Was she mad?"

"She was mad." I nodded, thinking about how hurt she'd been that I'd kept something so big from her. "She said all the same things that Jess and Claudia did. I swear, it's like girls have some kind of book they read out of. Then she reamed me for making her feel like she wasn't important enough to confide in."

Frank and Nick both opened their mouths, but before

they could say exactly what I had been thinking, I held up a hand.

"I know, I know. It's the exact opposite, and I tried to explain that to her, but she said after everything we went through and how we both almost died, we didn't get that luxury. We don't get to keep secrets and leave each other in the dark. She made me feel about yea big." I closed my finger and my thumb together until they were almost touching.

"They have a way of doing that, don't they?" Frank asked. "Claudia chewed my ass."

"I guess we had it coming." Nick dropped his chin into his hand like he was tired of waiting. "Speaking of, is this jackass ever gonna show up?"

The second the words left Nick's mouth, sunlight poured in through the front doors, followed quickly by the absence of it. The door slammed shut but no one walked through it, and the sound of thumps and shouting replaced the quiet.

My brothers and I hopped over the bar top and sprinted toward the door, unaware of what was happening on the other side of it. I tried to push it open, but it wouldn't budge.

"Something's blocking it," I exclaimed. "Help."

Frank and Nick both put their shoulders against the door, readying to push, but hard pounding came from the other side.

"Stop!" called a voice from outside the door. "It's the

police. Stop pushing."

We did as they asked and exchanged glances, dying for answers we didn't have.

"The police must have been waiting for him," Frank said.

"Maybe they know where the money came from?" Nick wondered out loud.

"Maybe they know who he is?" I added.

We moved away from the door and told the agitated customers who had gathered behind us that everything was fine. Pasting on big smiles, we offered everyone a drink on the house, which made them forget the entire ordeal. Free drinks tended to make people happy.

The door opened and the two police officers from last night walked in. Nick and Frank ushered them over to a quiet area of the bar while I finished making and serving the free drinks we'd promised our patrons.

Once I was free, I joined my brothers. "Fill me in," I said, wiping my hands on my towel.

One of the cops looked directly at me. "I was just telling your brothers that a member of the Luchessini mob family had been skimming off the top of his heists for years, back in the forties. Taking a little here and there and never getting caught. He got cocky. The only reason we have a record of any of this is because the items found in your safe were from just one heist, instead of smaller amounts from a bunch of them. You follow?" he asked me.

"Yeah, I follow."

"So this theft was so large that it ended up screwing the family he stole from for years. And it's how he got caught and eventually whacked by whoever he worked for. He wouldn't give up the location of the money and jewels, and they've been looking. All this time."

"It's been over seventy years, and they're still looking?" I asked, unable to believe it.

The cop nodded. "The story has been passed down through the generations. And each time someone new in the family hears the story, they start doing research and asking questions. Each one of them adds to the previous person's notes. It's extremely convoluted."

"So the guy outside . . ." Frank gestured toward the door. "Is he part of that family?"

"No," the cop said with a chuckle. "Which is crazy, right? He worked with some guys that Luchessini stole from originally. He knew that there was money hidden. He said he knew Sam Jr., and Sam recently confessed to him on his deathbed about the money being in the bar somewhere, but he wouldn't tell him where exactly."

"That's why he wanted to tear it down," I said, everything finally making sense.

"So, what happens now?" Frank asked.

The other cop chimed in. "We return the money to the rightful owners. The remaining living relatives in Vegas will be getting a rather large check and enough in jewels to provide for a lifetime. You'll be happy to know that the family needs it, and it will make a huge difference in their lives."

I smiled. "That does make me happy, actually." It wouldn't be satisfying to know that the money was going to someone who already had a fortune. I would have understood, though, because it had been theirs in the first place, but there was something about it actually making a difference that felt good.

"That guy isn't going to come after us, right?" Nick asked, frowning.

"Nah. You guys are fine. He only wanted the money, and you don't have that anymore."

"But he's going to jail because of us."

The cop shook his head. "He's going to jail for a long list of crimes that have nothing to do with you or this place. He won't be looking for revenge."

Despite the cop's certainty, it took everything in me to believe him.

After we shook hands with the policemen and signed our statements, one of them handed me a large envelope.

"The deed is in there," the cop said. "It's in pretty bad shape, so we put it in a protective sleeve. Make sure you file it with the county so something like this doesn't happen again."

I held the envelope gingerly as I extended it to Frank, who stood there with his hand out, waiting.

Frank grinned. "I'll take it to the courthouse."

LIFE CHANGES
Sofia

"**I**'M STILL MAD at you, you know," I said somewhat playfully as Ryan rubbed my back in bed, but I meant it.

I was still upset with him for keeping the situation with the bar from me the whole time he was going through it. I considered it my job to keep my man calm, to help carry his load, to shoulder his burdens with him. But I couldn't do any of those things if I didn't know he needed my help in the first place, if he didn't share his worries with me.

"I know." He pressed a kiss against my shoulder blade.

"Promise me you'll never keep things from me again," I said sternly, making him promise for what had to be the fifth time since he confessed it all to me.

He pressed another soft kiss to my back. "I promise."

I rolled over so I could look him in the eye. "You mean it?"

"Of course I mean it," he said solemnly.

I believed him, but I also knew it wouldn't be the last

time I asked. We women could be relentless that way.

Hope started to fuss, signaling she was awake. Right when I was about to get out of bed, Ryan stopped me.

"I'll get her."

He strode over to our daughter and leaned down, his chest and abs on full display as he picked her up. There was nothing sexier in the world than seeing the man you loved holding the child you'd created together. He rocked her back and forth, cradling her in his strong arms, and I melted a little at the sight. She looked so tiny next to him, like it wasn't possible that one day she would outgrow being held like that by him.

Ryan moved carefully toward our bed, his steps slow as he attempted to crawl back in. Hope cooed and stared up at him, her little fists clenching and unclenching as she turned her head toward Ryan's shirtless chest and tried to suckle.

"Not gonna happen, little angel." He moved her away with a laugh. "I don't have the right equipment," he added, handing her over to my waiting arms.

Each time I breastfed our daughter, Ryan watched like nothing had ever fascinated him more. And maybe nothing had? When you think about it, it's truly a miracle the things our bodies are capable of.

Hope eventually fell asleep, her head pressed against my breast, and Ryan told me he'd take her so I didn't have to get up. He scooped her carefully from my arms, her head supported just right as he laid her down gently in her bassinette.

"She still asleep?" I whispered.

"Didn't even move an inch," he said with a beautiful smile as I fought back a yawn. "Tired, angel?"

"Always," I said, and it was the truth. I'd forgotten how exhausting babies were.

The bed dipped as Ryan got back in and pulled me against his chest. With my back pressed against him, I snuggled in, loving the way his arms wrapped around me and held me tight. This man's arms were my home, a place I knew I'd always be safe, loved, and respected as long as I was in them.

About an hour later, I felt him stir, cool air hitting my body where his had just been, and it woke me momentarily. "You okay?" I asked, still mostly asleep.

"Just getting some water. You want some?"

"Huh-uh." I couldn't form any more words as I fell back to sleep. I didn't even remember him coming back to bed.

*

THE MORNING SUN peeked in through the blinds, and I cursed myself for forgetting to close them all the way last night. When I moved, I immediately felt it . . . a foreign weight on my hand that hadn't been there the night before.

Looking down, I felt my mouth drop open as I stared

at the diamond ring on my left hand.

"What is this? Ryan? Ryan, what is this?" I shook his shoulder but he refused to budge, his eyes closed tight, his breathing relaxed. So I pushed him back and forth forcefully, doing my best to get him to wake the hell up.

"What's wrong? Is the baby okay?" He shot up to a sitting position.

"The baby's fine. What the hell is this?" I shoved my hand in his face, and he gave me a cocky grin.

"Looks like an engagement ring to me," he said as he stretched his arms above his head.

"I know it's an engagement ring. Where did it come from?" I sputtered at him, half exasperated, half excited. I couldn't pick a single emotion; too many of them were running through me at once.

"A jewelry store. You can take it off, if you want."

"No." I yanked my hand back so quickly, he laughed.

"So you like it?"

I stared at the sparkling oval diamond surrounded by a circle of smaller diamonds, and practically swooned. "Like it? It's stunning."

"And the rose gold?" he asked, knowing how much I adored the flattering tone against my skin.

"It's unbelievable. Perfect."

Ryan smirked at me. "So you're going to keep it then?"

I wanted to smack him and kiss him at the same time. Staring at the ring on my hand, I waited for what felt like a full minute, but in my excitement, it was probably only about ten seconds.

"It depends," I said slowly, thinking that two could play this game, even though I knew I'd lose.

"Oh, it depends, huh?" He grinned and I nodded, trying to keep my expression serious. "On what exactly?" He reached for my hand.

"On your answer to my question."

"What question would that be?" His head cocked to the side, and his sly grin appeared again.

I held my hand in the air between us. "What's this ring doing on my finger?"

I kicked off the covers like I was about to storm out, but the truth was that I was hot. Had someone turned the heat on?

He climbed out of bed, then placed his hands on my legs and spun me to face him. "Waiting for you to finally say yes." He dropped to one knee.

"Yes to what?" I continued to toy with him as he reached for my left hand and pulled the ring off. I missed it instantly. With the ring now gone, my finger looked so sad and empty. I wanted to pout, but kept my mouth shut.

"To me, Sofia. Will you finally say yes to marrying me?" He held up the ring, his fingers dwarfing it. "Please say you'll be my wife. I can't wait any longer to make you mine."

"Of course I'll marry you."

He pushed the ring back on my finger, and the world righted itself again.

"I can't wait to be legally yours," I told him. "You know I already am in every other way."

I wrapped my arms around his neck and pulled his mouth to mine, our kiss slow, romantic, and deep.

HAPPY ENDING

Ryan

'D GROWN TIRED of waiting to put a ring on it, especially after Nick proposed to Jess.

I hated to admit it, but I was jealous of my little brother. And yes, I knew that I was the first Fisher to give our parents a grandbaby, and no one else had that going for them, but still. I wanted to be engaged and get married. Hell, I wanted it all . . . yesterday.

So while Sofia was passed out asleep—looking absolutely beautiful, I might add—I did what I'd tried to do once before. I put a ring on that otherwise empty finger. I figured if I wasn't supposed to ask her yet, then it wouldn't fit, just like it hadn't the last time I tried to slip it on.

But it did. It slipped right on, and I smiled to myself as I tried to fall back asleep, knowing what the coming morning would bring.

When she shook me awake like a combination between an earthquake and a thunderstorm, I'd forgotten for a second what I'd done. My heart raced with the worry that something bad had happened to Hope.

It wasn't until Sofia thrust her hand in front of my face, narrowly missing my nose, that I remembered what I'd done.

*

THREE WEEKS LATER, we gathered at the bar to welcome Frank and Claudia home from their honeymoon. We had started doing more family things at Sam's, even if it seemed like the least obvious place to do so. You'd be surprised at how family-friendly a bar could be when you were the one who owned it. To keep things legal, we got together when the bar wasn't open to the public so we weren't technically breaking any laws.

Frank and Claudia walked through the doors, glowing from their tans, and we all went crazy, shouting over one another and trying to get to them first.

Life was funny that way. You didn't always think you missed someone while they were gone, but the second you saw them again, it hit you just how much you did.

I suddenly felt like I had a million things to fill Frank in on, even though there actually was nothing new. And I wanted to hear all the details about their honeymoon in Tahiti. Well, not all the details, obviously, but they had stayed in one of those over-the-water bungalows, and I wanted to hear all about that, thinking that I could surprise Sofia with a trip there one of these days.

Frank's smile hadn't dimmed since they walked

through the doors, and I didn't know if it was because he was so relaxed, happy to see everyone, or for some other reason.

Nick appeared at my side and nudged my shoulder. "Why won't he stop smiling? It's freaky, right?"

I nodded. "I was just asking myself the same thing."

Frank headed toward us with that smile still plastered on his face. He pulled Nick and me into a group hug.

"Missed you guys," he said, sounding more like me than I did in the moment.

"Is that why you won't stop smiling?" Nick asked as we shoved him away.

"It's creepy. Please stop." I poked at Frank's cheek, and he slapped my hand away—hard.

"Not sure why I missed either of you jackasses," he growled, and before I could thank him for going back to normal, that damn smile reappeared. "You're going to be shitty uncles."

"What?" I sputtered as Nick said, "No way!"

"That took like two seconds." I shook my head, crazy excited that there would be another Fisher baby running around soon. "How do you know already?" I stepped behind the bar and poured us each a shot, then handed them out.

Frank shrugged as he reached for his glass. "We think she was pregnant before the wedding, actually. It's all Hope's fault."

I put my shot glass down and gave him a questioning

look. "How exactly is it my perfect angel baby's fault?

"Because," he said proudly. "I saw her and wanted one." He looked around and lowered his voice. "And then Claudia gave me *that look* when we got back home."

"What look?" Nick asked, leaning closer.

"The look that said she wanted one too." Frank said it in a way that made sure we knew that they were both to blame for this baby, and I bit back a laugh. "I told her I was going to put a baby in her, and she told me I'd better."

"Best getting-pregnant story ever." Nick lifted his shot glass in the air, and when he realized we weren't toasting yet, he set it back down.

"She basically threw down the gauntlet," I said, thinking how lucky they were that it worked out. It wasn't always that easy for most people to get pregnant.

"No shit. *I'd better.* Good thing I did." Frank's smile reappeared. "But I'm sure it didn't hurt that we've been trying ever since."

"Who else knows?" I asked.

"It's still so early," Frank said, "and she's nervous something could happen. But I'm sure by the end of today, everyone in this bar will know."

"You're going to be a dad." I slapped his back and squeezed his shoulder.

"I figured if you could do it, anyone could," he shot back.

We all laughed, raising our glasses. Then without a

word being spoken, Frank and I stared expectantly at Nick, who threw one hand in the air.

"We're not ready for kids yet, so stop giving *me* that look."

"But you're going to have kids, right?" I asked, realizing that none of us had ever talked about it. I'd always just assumed my brothers wanted the same things I did.

"Hell yes. I'll help populate the world with little Fishers at some point. Just not now."

His answer was good enough for me. "Here's to all the little Fishers . . . the ones on the way and the ones yet to come." I held my glass in the air, and we all clanked them together before downing our shots.

Life was good, and it was just getting started.

The End

Thank you so much for reading more about all the Fisher Brothers we've grown to love! I hope you enjoyed their story.

Have you read my other books? Flip to the next page to see a list of all the other series and stand-alone romance novels I've written. I'd love for you to meet everyone else.

Please join my mailing list to be notified of any new releases or sales. Trust me . . . you don't want to miss out! http://tinyurl.com/pf6al6u

OTHER BOOKS BY J. STERLING

In Dreams
Chance Encounters
10 Years Later – A Second Chance Romance
Daniel Alexander
Dear Heart, I Hate You

THE GAME SERIES
The Perfect Game – Book One
The Game Changer – Book Two
The Sweetest Game – Book Three
The Other Game (Dean Carter) – Book Four

THE CELEBRITY SERIES
Seeing Stars – Madison & Walker
Breaking Stars – Paige & Tatum
Losing Stars – Quinn & Ryson (Coming Soon)

THE FISHER BROTHERS SERIES
No Bad Days – Nick Fisher
Guy Hater – Frank Fisher
Adios Pantalones – Ryan Fisher

ABOUT THE AUTHOR

Jenn Sterling is a Southern California native who loves writing stories from the heart. Every story she tells has pieces of her truth in it, as well as her life experience. She has her bachelor's degree in Radio/TV/Film and has worked in the entertainment industry the majority of her life.

Jenn loves hearing from her readers and can be found online at:

Blog & Website:
www.j-sterling.com

Twitter:
twitter.com/RealJSterling

Facebook:
facebook.com/TheRealJSterling

Private Facebook Reader Group:
facebook.com/groups/ThePerfectGameChangerGroup

Instagram:
instagram.com/RealJSterling

If you enjoyed this book, please consider writing a spoiler-free review on the site from which you purchased it. And thank you so much for helping me spread the word about my books, and for allowing me to continue telling the stories I love to tell. I appreciate you so much. :)

Thank you for purchasing this book.

CPSIA information can be obtained
at www.ICGtesting.com
Printed in the USA
LVHW110040150119
603948LV00001B/48/P